RAINBOW MAN

RAINBOW MAN

DAVID W. BERNER

Writer Shed Press
www.writershedpress.com

Rainbow Man by David W. Berner
Published by Writer Shed Press

Clarendon Hills, Illinois
www.writershedpress.com

Copyright © 2022

All rights reserved. No portion of this book may be reproduced in any form without permission from the publisher, except as permitted by U.S. copyright law. For permissions contact: Writershedpress@gmail.com

Cover Art: *Melanie-at-Indalo-Art*

ISBN: 978-0-578-37996-8

Also by David W. Berner

Accidental Lessons

Any Road Will Take You There

Night Radio

A Well-Respected Man

Things Behind the Sun

Walks with Sam

For Leslie

"Do I dare disturb the universe?"

—T.S. Eliot

RAINBOW MAN

1

Robert wrecked the rental car. It skipped the curb and clipped a fire hydrant and the front bumper on the passenger side was bent several inches in toward the wheel well, a black rubber piece had torn away from the fiberglass. Fiberglass and rubber don't do well against cast iron. Robert recalled the day when a car's bumper was a *real* bumper, made of steel. There would have been little harm if carmakers hadn't become so cheap over the years, he thought. The damage wasn't terrible, and the car was drivable, but there it was anyway, damage to a car that wasn't his, a Chevy Impala that had been in his possession for less than a week. He now had to report what had happened but couldn't find the phone number for the rental car company. He believed the agent had written it on the outside of the contract envelope, and Robert thought he had tucked the paperwork under the visor. But in the minutes after the crash when he searched for it, it wasn't there. He pulled the car off the sidewalk and away from the hydrant, found the closest street parking, and sat inside, searching. He looked in the glove compartment, on the floor, and in the side pocket of the car's door. Nothing. Robert reached in the pocket of his windbreaker for his cell phone to call his daughter to alert her that he would be late, and there it was, the contract folded neatly in half. He made the phone call to the rental company. An agent was expected in an hour, and Robert would wait in the bar across the street.

Robert liked a beer now and then, but he wasn't much of a drinker, a few beers at the ball game was about it. He hadn't been inside Bigham Tavern since it changed hands. It was Kalb's for years. The new owners had spruced it up. Brought in some craft beer. They were serving wings now. The barstools were new. No more cracked vinyl. A beer sounded good, but with the rental car rep on his way, Robert had second thoughts. Still, he took a seat at the long bar.

"It's after the noon hour and it's *almost* five o'clock," the bartender said, smiling. He was a young man, about twenty-five or so, wearing a black Pirates cap, a large compass tattoo on his forearm.

"It's not about that, really," Robert said. "I had a little fender bender so I'm waiting for service."

"Ah, man. Are you okay?"

"It's minor."

The bartender slapped a cardboard coaster on the bar, one with the tavern's name on it. "You deserve a beer, I would say," he said.

"Car rental guy might smell it on me," Robert said.

"I'll vouch for ya."

The beer labels on the tap handles touted brews Robert had never heard of before—Fat Tire. Red Duck. Something called Vanilla Porter. He asked for a Rock, something familiar. They had it in bottles.

"Rolling Rock used to be brewed in Latrobe," Robert said. "Arnie's hometown."

A Pennsylvania hero, Arnold Palmer had lived his whole life in the small town where he grew up. He died there, too. The bartender had heard Arnie's story many times, mostly from out-of-towners who wandered in after stepping out to the viewing decks on Mt. Washington to see the glistening city lights below. He could pick out the tourists, always talking Western Pennsylvania trivia as if no one in the city had ever heard any of it before.

"How long you in town for?" the bartender asked.

"I live here. On Piermont. I was on my way to Greentree. My daughter lives there. Shoot," Robert said, remembering, "I still need to call her."

Robert took a sip from the green bottle.

He had been on his way to give Debbie the house key so she could retrieve his mail and the newspapers while he was away. He was one of the last on the street to have the *Pittsburgh Post-Gazette* delivered each day. It would be conspicuous if the papers were left to accumulate on the front walkway. It was Debbie's idea to come and get them, and it was Debbie who had questioned whether it was the best thing for her father to go overseas alone.

"Hey honey," Robert said into his phone. He explained the mishap, insisted he was fine, and told his daughter he wasn't sure when he'd be there. "It might take some time."

Debbie lived alone in the sprawling apartment complex along the Parkway West. She worked for Dick's Sporting

Goods at the corporate offices in Coraopolis. Robert didn't know exactly what it was she did, something to do with public relations or marketing or something like that, he believed. When she got the job after graduating from Pitt, Robert asked her if she knew the most famous person to come out of Coraopolis. Michael Keaton, she said, rolling her eyes.

"As soon as I get it straightened out, I'll call you. It was a dumb thing. Just hit the curb."

"And you're sure you're okay?"

"Fine. Not a big thing."

"Don't stand outside and wait. It's kind of chilly today. Can you go inside somewhere?"

"I'm inside. In Bigham. The bar. The place near me. Sorry to inconvenience you."

"It's okay, Dad. Please take your time. I'll wait for you. And be careful. You sure you don't want me to come? I can come."

"No. No. Don't worry, honey."

The images from three television sets above the bar flickered against the row of glasses on the back shelf. Each screen had been tuned to the same channel and the sound turned low.

"Pirates game last night. Big crowd," the bartender said.

"Still no player like Clemente," Robert said.

"Never saw him. Wasn't even born."

"Best ever."

"I hear that a lot."

"At the game a few days ago. Used to go a lot more than I do now. It'd been a long time. Bucs won. But I lost."

"How's that?"

"I usually take the incline and the bus, you know? This time, though, I thought I'd drive. But the guy in the parking lot hit me. The back of the car. Big hurry. He wasn't looking. That's why I have that rental. My car's in the shop."

"You've had some car issues, my friend."

"You could say that."

"Your insurance taking care of it, right?"

"It's going to be several days to repair and I'm heading across the pond. They can keep it for a while."

Robert lifted the beer bottle to his lips and before tasting, he said, "Spain. I'm going to Spain."

It had been years since Robert had taken a trip of any kind. The summer before Debbie went to high school, the family had traveled to Nag's Head for a week, and there was the tenth anniversary trip to Florida, but there had been nothing since, nothing of significance. The only other trips were the seasonal drives with Emma near Seven Springs in the fall to see the leaves. A few months after Emma was gone, Debbie tried to get him to go to Cook Forest for a weekend in the woods, maybe some fishing, a trip together where she could watch over him. It would do him good, she said. Good for her, too. But Robert wasn't interested. He used to like fishing. He once liked going down to the river on early Saturday mornings. Debbie offered a trip to New York, too. They could see *Hamilton*, she said. It didn't happen. It was a year before Robert returned to the ballpark. Leaving the house for anything had been difficult for some time. It was a good house, a good place to hide. He and Emma had lived in the little three-bedroom for thirty years. They bought it a few years after the wedding when Robert had landed the manager job at Giant

Eagle. They raised their daughter there, he mowed the small lawn, planted a Japanese maple near the front door stoop, and together they walked as a family to St. Mary's on Grandview on summer Sundays. After Emma, the house, so empty and quiet, had become Robert's cocoon. Years later, on a morning in February, he awakened to a bitter wind and big snowfall. Robert stayed in bed, drinking coffee, and reading as the snow piled up. As a New Year's resolution, he had made a list of books he'd never read but thought he should now that he had the time. It was one of several lists Robert had compiled to jump-start the new year, jump-start him. There was one on movies and a list of card games he had never learned to play. Bridge had always seemed so complicated. There was the flower list, too, plants he had always wanted to try to grow— roses and orchids. Robert had begun to tackle the book list, books that had seemed out of reach. He jumped into *War and Peace* and gave up; *Ulysses* and gave up. On that snowy morning it was *The Sun Also Rises,* and for whatever reason that clicked. He read all day and finished it that night. The next day he could think only of *Spain.* The months alone, the isolation falling away after reading Hemingway's romantic words—the wine, the fishing, and the glorious fiestas. A different world, a new world. Robert couldn't explain it. Why that book? Why Spain? Most of the book takes place in Paris. Why not Paris? For whatever reason, the chapters on Spain were what hooked him. Robert booked a two-week trip. Spain in the summer. Spain by himself. It all happened just like that.

"Now there's a trip that sounds amazing," the bartender said. "You must be retired?"

"A few years now," Robert said.

"Taking your wife?"

Robert had wondered on the day he'd booked his flight: *Would Emma have wanted this trip the way I do?* She, too, had never been overseas. Long ago when they were young and dating, they took weekend drives to Lake Erie and spent their days on the beach at Presque Isle. They ate fried fish sandwiches; he drank beer and she sipped white chilled wine at the little restaurant near the beach with the white fence around it and the outside tables near a grove of trees. In Spain, Robert thought, Emma could have sat by the sea, drinking white sangria.

"No. Only me," Robert answered.

He took another swig of Rock, leaving a bit in the bottle, wiped his lips with a bar napkin, and looked toward the door, as if he had anticipated someone walking through it. He placed a five-dollar bill on the table.

"That'll do it, right? Little tip there, too."

"You are good, my friend."

"I better wait by the car," Robert said.

The bartender removed the empty bottle and swiped a white cloth across the bar. "Always wondered about what a bullfight was really like," he said.

It wasn't long before the Avis agent arrived. He inspected the car, asked Robert some questions, and had him fill out paperwork. Robert had agreed to the extra rental insurance when he was handed the keys. It seemed a good thing to do and it turned out it had been. Since the crash was minor, the agent told him to keep the car through the contract's end. Robert was scheduled to return it in two days. Pulling away to his daughter's place, the bells of St. Mary rang out, signaling the end of Saturday evening mass. And when he stopped at the corner, Robert saw the bartender standing outside the entrance to Bigham, his back to the wall, cigarette smoke rising above his head.

"I want to hear some stories about matadors!" the bartender shouted.

Robert wasn't sure about a bullfight. Not sure he could stomach it. Still, coming home with a story or two to tell the bartender would be nice, a story or two to tell his daughter, too. Maybe not tales of bulls and red capes and swords, but memorable stories, nonetheless. Robert hoped to take photos so he could remember those stories, and Debbie had showed him how to work the camera on his phone. He had been practicing taking pictures of the city from Grandview Avenue.

Robert drove down the hill toward the boulevard and onto the Parkway toward his daughter's apartment. He reminded himself to pack a second bottle of antacids for his trip, another suggestion from Debbie. She worried about his touchy stomach. Robert couldn't recall if he'd put his new passport, the only one he'd ever had, in the side pocket of his suitcase at home or if it was still on the kitchen table where he'd placed the boarding pass for his flight and the hotel reservation confirmation he had printed from the computer. When he returned home, he'd be sure to check for the passport. And he would check again in the morning and on his way to the airport, double and triple and quadruple check. Of all the things to forget, that would be the worst. His daughter had said he'd been a little forgetful lately. Maybe she was right.

2

It was St. Augustine, the anniversary trip. That was the last time Robert had been on a plane. This flight would not only be the first since then, but it would be the longest plane ride of his life, and much of it, nearly all of it, over water.

How do they keep this thing in the air?

The flight attendant was a pretty woman with an olive complexion, deep brown hair pulled back in a tight ponytail, and dressed in a military-style uniform—dark blue, shoulder straps, and fake brass buttons.

"Sir, you are sitting in an emergency exit row and in the event that anything goes wrong, it is likely we will need your assistance. Are you okay with this, sir?"

Robert thought how odd it was that the attendant was smiling when she explained potential disaster.

"In the event of an emergency, it is possible that a flight attendant may not be able to assist in opening these exit doors. We may be helping other passengers. So, it's important that you know how to properly operate them."

The attendant noted the instructions posted on the door and asked that Robert read them. It was then that a large man, after stuffing a soft leather bag into the overhead, fell into the aisle seat in Robert's two-seat row.

"I know how this works," the man said to the attendant. He turned toward Robert. "I always request these seats. More leg room, am I right?"

The attendant completed her explanation and asked both Robert and his seatmate to pay close attention to the safety guidelines when it came time for her to announce them.

The man gave the attendant a thumbs-up.

"George," the man said, offering his hand to Robert. "Another business trip for me. Hate these things. Especially the long ones. Been doing it for a long time. Getting old. But you gotta do what you gotta do, right? Company used to give me first class. Not anymore. All the cutbacks."

The man buckled his seatbelt. Robert did the same.

"And you, what's your story?" the man asked.

My story? Robert paused, took a breath, and thought for a moment. "Spain. I guess that's my story."

"Good thing," the man laughed, "this plane's going straight to Madrid."

The first leg was to New York, but Robert knew what he meant.

"It's something I wanted to do," Robert said.

Those words sounded strange to Robert. A trip he wanted to do. That's not true. Spain was more of an impulse, a yearning sparked by a good book.

"I made this list of things, you see. Things to do in my older years. Things I never got to. I read some Hemingway, and here I am."

"Are you running with the bulls?" the man asked, knowing it couldn't be true.

Robert laughed. "I would certain be killed. Think that might be a bit too much excitement for me. Going to the south. Granada. I hear it's wonderful."

"Spain is a good place," the man said, tucking a navy-blue neck pillow behind his head and leaning against the seat. "Good food. Wine. You know about tapas?"

"Little bites?"

"A lot of it is free. Many times, they'll keep feeding you as long as you keep drinking."

"Well, I like a little wine. But maybe not that much."

"Spain is going to change your mind about that. It does that, Spain. Changes minds."

Out the window, Robert saw the ground crew moving the last of the luggage from a motor cart to a conveyor belt and into the plane's belly. He looked for his suitcase but didn't see it and that worried him a little. Robert closed his eyes and leaned his head on the window. He tried to remember a prayer his mother used to recite when he would go to bed, a prayer to his Guardian Angel, his little body under the covers and his mother sitting beside him with her hands clasped.

* * *

It was impossible to sleep on the flight, despite the crew trying its best to help—dimming the lights, pulling all the window shades down. Robert ate the baked chicken and russet potatoes and vanilla pudding, balancing it all as best he could on the tray table. He thought maybe an after-dinner drink of whiskey and ginger ale would help. He hadn't had a real cocktail in years. But this was vacation, and it might knock him out. It didn't. Ten dollars was a lot of money, he thought, for an ineffective sleeping pill. So, he watched a movie—*The Surprise*—Norwegian or Swedish, maybe, with subtitles. It was a comedy about two people who sign a contract to end their lives and then fall in love and change their minds. It was oddly dark and oddly amusing. He read a bit, too, one of Rick Steve's guidebooks about the south of Spain, a bit of *The Sun Also Rises*, returning to pages he had dogeared, and *For Whom the Bell Tolls*. He had carried all three on board, all old paperbacks. He read the section in the guide on the food and wines of Granada and Ronda, the chapters on the travels to Pamplona in *Sun*, and the last pages of *Bell*. He had loved the book's ending—another novel on his list that he had finally conquered—beautifully written despite the machismo that runs through all the sentences. And, of course, the hero carried his name—Robert. But what Robert wasn't prepared for was how much that ending—one of sacrifice, lost love, and death—would distress him in the second reading, flying high above the Atlantic.

Robert ordered another whiskey despite his better judgment and asked the flight attendant when they might be landing.

"Our arrival time in Madrid is in about three hours. Can I get you anything else?"

Robert shook his head, placed a paper napkin on his tray and lifted the clear plastic cup to his mouth.

"Should have ordered some red wine," his seatmate said. The man shifted in his seat and opened one eye. He could see the tea-like color of the liquid in Robert's glass. "You're going to Spain, remember," the man added.

"I'm sure I'll have my fill. I might become a lush." Robert lifted his glass in a mock toast.

"You'll be sending a case or two of red wine home before you leave. I guarantee it. You better try to get some shuteye, my friend."

The seatmate adjusted his neck rest and closed his eyes.

The man's suggestion sounded like something Debbie would have said. Since her mother's death, she had been tirelessly looking after her father. Did you take your antacids? Did you make that dentist appointment? Are you eating, Dad? You must eat. She meant well. Still, many times this made Robert feel like a child, had him questioning his abilities and his mental state, something he didn't want to think about. Was he losing it? He was older, yes, but he wasn't helpless. When he told her about the trip, Debbie was full of concerns. All by yourself? Are you sure? Why are you doing this? You'll get lost, Dad. You're an old man. You know how you are with directions. Maybe you should go with a senior group, one of those guided bus tours with people your age. Wouldn't that be a better idea? Wouldn't that make more sense? In time, she stopped asking. Although he knew Debbie's worrying wouldn't end.

With the lights still dimmed and only whispered voices to hear, Robert swallowed what remained of his drink and made a silent salute to his daughter.

* * *

It was the announcement to return to your seats and buckle seatbelts that had awakened Robert. The second whiskey had helped, but now the plane was close to landing, below 10,000 feet and beginning its descent to Madrid.

"Ladies and gentlemen, we will be landing shortly," the pilot said over the speakers. "The local time is 9:35. The weather is good. It's a nice morning in Madrid. Clear skies and 18 degrees. We appreciate you flying with us. Welcome to Spain."

Robert's seatmate drank from his coffee. "You missed breakfast," he said. "It wasn't much. A muffin in a plastic wrapper. And this." He raised his coffee cup.

"Not sure I'm ready to eat. But coffee, maybe," Robert said, adjusting his seat to the upright position.

"They won't get you any now."

"I'll grab one at the airport."

"You like espresso?"

"I've had it, I think. Strong, right?"

"Espresso is kind of the thing here."

"Heavy."

"I love it. But it's an acquired taste."

"When in Spain."

"You should get a hat, too. One of those straw ones."

Robert had never been much of a hat guy, except his old Bucs baseball cap.

"A requirement in Spain?" Robert asked.

The seatmate lifted his eyes to Robert's hairline. "People wear hats. You could use one. Not to be too forward, but there's some skin up there."

Robert still had some hair, but it had thinned a good deal in the last few years. He had given up trying to cover the bald spot on his crown and was keeping his hair trimmed more closely. He had gone to the same barber, Stanley on Southern Avenue, for decades. Sat in the same chair, usually on a Saturday. But when Stanley's hands started to shake, Robert switched to the shop on Grandview. He had been troubled by the change. Stanley had been a friend. Robert didn't know the name of a single barber in the new place. They were always coming and going.

"Hats are everywhere," the seatmate continued. "Airport shops will have them to buy. You can get a decent one for a few euros. You'd look good in one."

Robert wasn't sure about that.

"Spain can get hot," the man said. "The sun shines all the time."

"A hat and an espresso."

"There you go." The seatmate lifted his coffee cup in a toast. "To España!"

Robert had purchased a little translation book at the airport before the flight. He had wanted to study it during the journey but had forgotten. There would be two hours at the Madrid airport before his bus was scheduled to leave and then five hours to Granada. He could teach himself a few things along the way, at least some of the essentials. Where's the bathroom? *Something—baño—right?* Robert studied two years of Spanish in high school, but that was a lifetime ago. And as it always goes, you lose it if you don't use it. He had heard that many Spaniards spoke English, but he didn't want to be the ugly American. So, he bought the book, and he would study and listen to conversations of the passengers on the long bus ride, and he would whisper new words to himself several times over until they felt comfortable. And when he would arrive in Granada, he would hail a taxi like a Spaniard, wearing the new straw hat he bought for 20 euros at one of those little shops in the airport terminal.

3

The door to the hotel was made of heavy wood, thick and deep brown, and recessed in the building's white sandstone. It was late when Robert arrived, sometime after 10 p.m. His attempt at Spanish had sent the cab driver from the bus station to the wrong hotel. The driver threw his hands in the air in frustration when Robert realized the first hotel wasn't the right one. There are two, he learned. Isabella and Isabel. One is a queen, one a saint. Robert's rough Spanish had navigated the cabbie to the "queen" in the busy part of the city. He wanted the "saint" up the narrow streets to the hills of Albaicín.

Centuries ago, the Hotel Santa Isabel la Real had been someone's home. A few small rooms surrounded a tiled courtyard. Robert's room was on the first of two floors. The caretaker, an older woman, nodded as Robert greeted her in English. She gave him his key and showed him his room of white linens and mahogany furniture.

Robert placed his bag on the bed.

"Tapas?" he asked.

"Sí, señor. San Miguel, the plaza," the woman said.

"Can I walk?"

"Sí."

The woman motioned for Robert to follow, walked him out the main door, and pointed down the dark cobblestone road.

"Dos minutos," she said.

Robert changed his shirt, brushed his teeth, and threw water on his face. He was tired but hungry and wondered what might be available to eat at such a late hour, on such a hot night, in a plaza near a church in a quiet neighborhood overlooking the city.

Robert had read about the late diners in Spain, but he never expected the tiny restaurants in the Plaza de San Miguel to be so busy, many of the patrons were regulars, it seemed, with a few scattered tourists. He heard a smattering of French and German, but most were fast-talking Spaniards who seemed to know each other. He took an outside table at Bar Lara with a view of the church and its grand wooden double-doors at the top of the stone steps, a few feet from the large public crucifix.

"Hola," the waitress said. "Algo para beber?"

The phrase was not familiar, not anything Robert had read in his little book on the bus. A bit confused, but understanding the usual ritual, he assumed the waitress was asking what he might wish to drink.

"Sí. Ah, roja?"

"Red wine?" The waitress had learned to spot an American. "I speak English," she said.

Robert was surprised by her accent. Maybe a hint of the American South. She was an unremarkable woman, the kind that would not necessarily attract attention. Robert guessed she was in her early 40s. Thin with ballerina shoulders. Her hair was short like a boy's, dark, nearly black, and delicately flecked with gray. She wore silver earrings that dangled to her cheekbones. No noticeable make-up. Large eyes that lingered on their target a moment longer than most.

"Oh, that's good. I just got here. Not sure I'm ready to try to tackle the language full on. I have this." Robert produced the translation book.

"You're in luck," she said. "Will you be eating?"

"Sí."

"Aquí está el menu de tapas. Tome su tiempo."

Robert shrugged.

"I'm just playing with you. I'll bring a menu and that red wine. Grenache okay?"

It was still warm under the stars after a day of near 37-degree temperatures, 100-degrees Fahrenheit, by Robert's calculation. He was proud that he was at least *thinking* in Celsius. Meters and kilometers would come later. He leaned back in his chair and breathed deeply, trying to settle in after the long travel. He swallowed one antacid tablet and remembered he had promised to phone Debbie, tell her he had made it safe and sound.

"Here you are," the waitress said, placing the stemmed glass and a menu on the table.

"Do you know what time it is in the U.S?" Robert asked.

"They are six to seven hours behind. What city?"

"Eastern time zone there. Pittsburgh?"

"Six. I knew some people in Georgia."

Robert now understood the accent.

"So, then, it's what?" He studied his wristwatch.

"Five in the afternoon," she said.

"I need to call my daughter. Got the international plan while I'm here," Robert said, removing his cellphone from the front pocket of his pants.

"Good idea," she said. "I'll give you some time with the menu and bring some tapas in a moment. You know it's free, right?"

"I heard that. But I have to keep drinking."

"And the problem with that is?" The waitress laughed and touched Robert's shoulder. "The menu, it has a lot of choices. I can help if you need it."

"Gracias, senora."

"Nice. So far so good on the Spanish." The waitress winked and turned toward the door to the small kitchen.

There was a particular way he was to dial his phone to make a call back home. *The number 1 first? No. There's some country code, right? Zero, 1. No. Zero, zero 1?* For several minutes Robert dialed one combination and another. He heard only a fast busy each time.

The waitress placed a small plate in front of Robert. Green olives around tiny pieces of bread with thinly sliced cured ham on top, and a cut of cheese.

"This is manchego. You get a lot of that while you're here. I assume you haven't been in Spain before."

"Looks wonderful," Robert said, moving his wine closer to the plate.

"I can always tell the first timers," she said.

Robert continued to fiddle with his phone. "I'm sure you have called someone back in Georgia."

"Not really."

"I can't get through," he said.

"Not sure there's anyone that wants to hear from me as much as your daughter wants to hear from you," she said. The waitress gestured toward Robert's phone. "Can I help?" she asked.

Robert watched as she typed in numbers. He noticed a bright silver ring on her index finger, her nails plain and unpainted.

"And your daughter's number?"

Robert offered it. He had kept it on a small piece of paper in his wallet. Not that he couldn't remember his own daughter's number. He just didn't want to forget it.

The waitress dialed, dialed again, and listened. "It's going through," she said. "I've learned a bit about international calling working here, helping tourists like you."

Several rings and Debbie answered.

"Dad? Hello?"

"Hold on for your father," the waitress said. She smiled and handed the phone to Robert.

Robert said he was sorry it took so long to call. There were some problems with the cab ride, he told Debbie, and he had forgotten the codes for dialing, and he was only now settling in. Debbie asked about the woman on the phone. A nice waitress who had helped, Robert told her.

"She's from Georgia, I think," Robert said.

Robert looked up from his phone, but the waitress had walked away to another table where a young couple sat with two wine bottles on the table.

"The first waitress I get in Spain and she's from America. Small world, huh?"

Robert took a sip of his wine.

Debbie questioned why his father had allowed a stranger to handle and dial his phone.

"Oh, honey, she's nice. And trying to help. She got me through to you. I was doing a bad job of it."

"You need to be careful, Dad."

Robert swallowed another sip of wine.

"I will," he said. "Promise. I just wanted you to know I was here and safe." Robert liked hearing his daughter's voice, as if she were only a short drive away.

"I love you too, sweetheart," he said.

It was close to midnight in a lovely Spanish neighborhood on a hill, but Robert wasn't quite in the swing of it yet—this vacation, this adventure. Long travel, time changes, and the misdirected cab had tempered his arrival. And although the waitress was sweet and welcoming, and the wine and food were much needed, there was a long way to go before he would and could let Spain sink in. It was thousands of miles from Pittsburgh, and far too early to expect much. Still, he believed it was, all-in-all, a good start, and his American encounter had made him feel less alone in a big world.

"Have you decided?" the waitress said, returning to his table.

"Your name," Robert said. "May I ask?"

"Chloe."

"I'm Robert." He offered his hand. "Hola, Chloe. Chloe from Georgia."

Robert had come to Spain for reasons he had not yet completely calculated—to revitalize something, to renew something, to forget something, to find one last adventure, to discover a new sensation for long lingering emotions. Maybe it was a little of everything. Granada was a beautiful city in one of the most vibrant countries in Europe, and there he was, enlivened yet tentative.

"Another glass of wine?" Chloe asked.

Robert thought for a moment and smiled. "Sí, mi amiga."

Spain might lead him to both the places he wanted and needed to go, he thought, but it would take space and time to acclimate to its ways, including its long days of sun and its measured pace. Spain might make him stronger than he had been in a long while, since happier days, since Emma. It would ease him into a new life or throw him. Either way, he was going to find out and he had convinced himself that he was ready for it. Is there nothing to lose? He tried not to think about that.

4

Albaicín's ancient roads were not built for modern taxis. Nor were they built for mini-buses, mini-vans, or crowds of pedestrians, certainly not all at once. Robert had been warned to open the hotel door to the street with caution. On his walk toward the plaza on his way to the city center, he found himself hugging the building walls as cars passed. Drivers beeped their horns and slowed down and waited for the walkers to place themselves against the sandstone or slip into a narrow entrance of a home as the autos rushed by.

Robert carried a paper map he had been given at the hotel. With the ink of a blue pen, the caretaker had circled several locations for the first day in Granada. Robert walked down the winding, tumbling streets to the Moorish market near the Cathedral de Granada. He took photos with his phone. The streets were lined with spices and teas, handmade scarves, and colorful ceramic pots and cups. He was told it would be best to haggle and negotiate prices, but instead he smiled and bought a small bag of saffron at the price that was asked. Robert knew he could do nothing with it during his days in Spain; he wasn't going to cook, certainly, and he wasn't sure what to do with saffron anyway. It was the spice's aroma that captured him. *It smells like Spain*, he thought. The vendor urged Robert to taste it. "Bueno. Muy bueno." Bitter but sweet, like natural honey. Tasting the spice was like tasting a flower.

On the steps outside the cathedral, three nuns in traditional habits walked slowly toward the massive arched wooden door, speaking softly in Spanish. Two old women handed out red carnations and asked for money. Robert had been told to smile and say, "No gracias." He had to say it three times but was sorry he had to say it at all. Inside the cathedral, hushed voices echoed off the Corinthian columns lining the main aisle. The Gothic Portal, hand-carved religious figures—Saint Michael and the Three Wise Men—appeared to protect those who had come to see it all. And kneeling in one of the wooden pews closest to the aisle was one of the nuns he had noticed outside. She was slight, young, a smaller woman than the other sisters. Her complexion was that of a child, eyes alert. She noticed Robert as she looked up from her prayers, offered a bowed head, and smiled. He returned the same but quickly looked away, embarrassed he may have interrupted her devotions.

"Señor," she whispered.

From her kneeling position, the young nun signaled Robert with her eyes. Robert pointed to his chest and stepped toward her.

"Has venido aquí para estar con Dios?" she asked.

In Catholic grade school where Robert had attended, only nuns taught the students. No lay teachers. And it was in that school that he had learned that guilt was an acquired emotion, always under the surface of his skin, waiting. That old guilt had surfaced now. He had intruded and he was being summoned.

"Por Dios?" she asked again.

"Habla Inglés?" Robert asked.

"Are you here for God?" the young nun translated.

Robert held silent then thought for a moment.

"I am on vacation, sister. On holiday."

"Many are," she said. "They come to see this magnificent place. But you, you are here for more?"

Robert looked toward the altar. Sunlight beamed through the arched windows high above it.

"I was raised Catholic. Go to church at home. So, maybe? Maybe, yes. I'm not sure."

"I watch you. You step with light feet. You are uncertain, no?"

Robert rubbed the back of his neck and looked again to the altar. It was if he had been caught in a sin, as if the nun had the eyes of God.

"I am a little uncomfortable, sister," he said.

"I do not mean to make you feel this way," she said. "Sometimes, I feel these things. I cannot ignore them. Forgive me."

She stood and stepped from the pew to the aisle.

"Oh no. Please," Robert said, apologizing for something unknown.

"It has happened before," she said. "I see someone. They are searching. Again, I am sorry. It is the curse of my profession. No?"

"Yes," Robert said. "Profession. A calling."

The young nun made the sign of the cross.

"La paz sea con vosotros," she said.

Robert's face softened, as if resigning himself to a state of being.

"Peace. Peace be with you," the young nun said in English.

She touched Robert's hand, and for what seemed a long moment, she held her eyes on him, and stepped away, walking toward the altar, disappearing through a nearby door.

All around him, Robert could see the opulence of religious grandeur, the ancient weight of man's offerings to God. He moved himself into the middle of the pew, lowered the kneeler, and lowered himself. He closed his eyes. The hundreds of Hail Marys and Our Fathers he had recited over the decades seemed not to have been enough.

* * *

It was mid-afternoon, and Robert needed a break from the sun. He had spent much of the day walking in and out of the shops in what one brochure had called Little Morocco. He drank mint tea from inside one of the few air-conditioned cafes, and from his vantage point watched a woman with a British accent haggle with a shop owner over the price of a rose-colored scarf. Robert was fascinated with two young men smoking hookah in an open-air restaurant across the narrow street. *Should I try that?* he thought. Robert had not walked so much in one day in a long time. The heat had withered him, so there was no reason to hurry through his time with the tea and the cool air. Robert's only remaining plan for the day was tapas at Bodegas Casteñada, a spot he had read about in a travel brochure or book and believed he would regret if missed.

"Señor, more tea?" the woman asked, almost too softly to detect. She wore a sundress of orange, the tattoo of a star on her bare shoulder.

"Gracias," Robert said.

"Mint, señor?" she asked, reminding herself.

Robert could see on a small shelf behind the woman there was an array of small teapots and cups, each alive in shades of blue, purple, and red. The woman noticed Robert's attention to them.

"Beautiful, no?" she asked.

"Beautiful," Robert said. "Something for my daughter, maybe."

He stood to get a closer look.

"Sí. Traditional Moroccan," the woman said.

From a lower shelf, Robert removed a small pot.

"She would love this," he said.

The body of the pot was a marbled shade of sapphire with the bottom and top edges in bright green. The handle was delicately curved and made of sandalwood, and the long spout was the color of rose. Tied to the lid was a bright red tassel.

"Muy agradable," the woman said.

Emma, like Debbie, had loved her tea, steeping the leaves and spices in an old white ceramic teapot she been given as a gift on her birthday one year. After dinner, the perfume of herbs would fill the kitchen. And now, Robert detected the scent of cinnamon inside the shop, like the caramel apple herbal tea that Emma regularly bought from a little tea store on the city's South Side.

"That's lovely," Robert said. He looked toward the shop's counter and the closed door behind it. "Is someone else making tea?

"Señor?"

Robert waved his hand near his face, calling the aroma to him.

"I smell it. Is someone drinking another kind of tea somewhere?"

"No. You are alone, señor. No one else. Only you and me."

"Yes. Yes, of course," he said, taking another look around the small shop.

"And this, will you have it?" the woman asked, raising the teapot to eye level.

"Sí," Robert said. "Can you wrap it, carefully, por favor?"

"Por supuesto."

Robert returned to his seat and finished his tea.

* * *

Jamón hung in a long row from a rack above the bar. Waiters in white aprons rushed from the kitchen door, nearly colliding with each other, and the sound of clinking wine glasses and fast-talking locals was all around, laughter and cheers bouncing off the framed mirrors and the tiled walls. The air was infused with olive oil. An enormous bull's head hung on a far wall. Robert had been told of a Spaniard's passions—wine and food and friends. That mixture was in full view, the vitality deafening. Without standing or stepping from his small round table in the corner, sitting still in observation, Robert's muscles ached as if he had walked the slopes of a mountain. The energy of Bodegas Casteñada could wear one out.

"Otra sangria?" The waiter asked, bounding before Robert with nervous vigor.

Robert wasn't certain what he had been asked but accepted that his nearly empty glass with melting ice and tiny pieces of fruit at the bottom would have prompted a refill, so he nodded.

"Oh, and the, ah, ensalada rusa?" he asked, searching for the right words.

Robert was on his fourth tapas—ham and tomatoes, some concoction of shrimp and mussels, and pork and onions. His third sangria was now on the way.

At the bar, a woman clutched the arm of a man. She sat on a stool, and he stood, leaning into her. She kissed him, once and then again, on the lips and below his ear. She whispered something, smiled, and moved her fingers under the waistband of his pants above the back pocket of his jeans. She kissed him again, this time on the cheek. She flipped her dark brown hair from her eyes and kissed him once again. Robert tried not to watch, but it was impossible. The affection, the sensuality had an extraordinary intoxication even in the company of strangers. Robert looked and then looked away, and in an attempt not to be noticed, he turned his attention to his phone. On the screen was a notification. There was a voicemail from his daughter. Robert tried to listen, but the clatter was too much.

The waiter placed the glass of sangría on Robert's table. "Ensalada en un momento," he said and turned away.

The woman with the man caught Robert's eye and lifted her bottle of cerveza in a toast. Robert raised his glass. *What would Emma have thought of this place? This woman? How much I've had to drink? It was late afternoon in Pittsburgh. Debbie would be getting home from work about now. I should call.* Robert took two long drinks. If he left the table, it would be snatched up quickly by one of the dozens who stood at the busy bar.

"Excuse me, ah, excusa," Robert said.

The woman with the man stood and moved slightly toward Robert.

"My table. Can you watch my table?" he asked, pointing to his seat and his phone.

"No Ingelés," she said. "Haz una llamada?" The woman held her hand to her ear as if making a phone call.

"Yes," Robert said. "Can you watch my table?"

The woman said something to the man, and he turned to Robert and nodded. The couple, carrying their cervezas, moved to Robert's table. The woman clinked her bottle against Robert's glass.

"Sin preocupaciones," she said.

The small outside patio with its tables tightly arranged was alive with patrons. Robert moved along the alley to the entranceway of a now closed bookstore to find a less hectic spot.

"Dad?" Debbie answered. "Dad, are you okay?"

"Yes, honey, I wanted to check in."

"It must be late there, right? You're all right?"

"I'm at a wonderful place, honey," Robert said. "Sorry. It's kind of loud. Can you hear me?" He stepped around the corner of the building at the end of the alley.

"Where you are?"

"A tapas bar. It's so alive. It's almost unnerving. But it's good. It's good, really."

"Are you getting around okay?"

"A lot of walking." Robert turned his back to a momentary burst of revelry. "Oh, hold on a sec." He moved the phone from one ear to the other. "Can you still hear? Is that better?"

"It sounds kind of wild there."

"The people are so, I don't know, in love with life. Yes, that's it. In love with life."

"Are you drinking?"

"I've had some sangria."

"Dad. You have to be careful."

"Honey, I'm good. Feel good, really."

"I know I talked to you yesterday. But I like you checking in like this."

"You know, I think your mother would have loved it here. I bought you something today."

"You don't need to do that."

"You'll love it."

"Is it hot there? It must be hot."

"Sun never stops shining. Your mother would be wearing a big hat. There are a lot of hats here."

"I tried to reach you earlier today. When you don't answer it makes me anxious."

"It's okay. Really. But I should go, honey. Some nice people are watching my table in the bar. I just wanted to be sure you knew I was all right."

"People?"

"Nice young couple."

"Okay. Be sure to get your sleep. Be careful going back to your room. This call is probably costing you a fortune."

When Robert returned to the bar, the couple was gone. At his table now were four young women, maybe in their 20s, a pitcher of sangria sat in the center. The women laughed and spoke fast and furiously in Spanish. Robert stood before them, uncertain of what to do.

"Ah señor! Your table, no?"

"Yes, I was making a call." He made the phone gesture to his ear.

"Si, si. This for you. The man and the woman. They gave this gift." The woman handed Robert a tall, fresh glass of sangria.

"The couple?" Robert asked.

"Si. They had to go. Mucha prisa."

"They bought this for me?"

"They were sorry," the young woman said. "Please, sit. Be with us." She pointed to an empty chair one of her friends had commandeered and added to their group. "You are American, no? We love to talk to Americans."

The women clinked their glasses and laughed.

Hours passed. More sangria, and several plates of tapas. When the women called Robert a taxi, one hugged him goodbye and helped him to the cab's rear seat. All four threw kisses as the taxi drove away. Robert waved from the window.

"Bar Lara, por favor," he said to the driver. "It's in the plaza near the hotel named after the saint, not the queen. And the plaza is, yes, San Miguel? Yes, Plaza de San Miguel."

5

Steps from the church, a man played the fiddle, the music drifting over the tables in the warm air. It was after midnight, not all the plaza tables were taken as they might have been earlier. Robert found a table near a small tree. He was tired, lightheaded, drunk, and unable to wind down from the night. He wanted coffee.

"My friend. How are you?" Chloe's greeting startled Robert. He turned toward her voice.

"Hola. I am good," Robert said. "It's so nice to see you again."

Chloe stood at Robert's chair. "Well," she said, "it's clear you've had an interesting night."

"I might have had some sangria."

"Oh, Robert. As they say, do as the Romans."

"The Spaniards."

"What will it be? Are you still celebrating?" Chloe asked.

"I believe it's time to come down from the night."

"If you are in Spain, as you are, I would suggest an espresso."

"I've been told this. But what about the caffeine? Will I sleep?"

"French press coffee has more caffeine than an espresso."

"And there is no decaffeinated espresso, right?"

"Don't say that too loud. Spaniards will laugh at you."

"There's a double espresso, right? That's what they're called?"

"I have something better. Might go down easier. A double cortado."

"And that is?"

"Espresso shots and a little steamed milk on the top. I think it'll help fight off the coming hangover. And it definitely is coming." Chloe playfully tapped Robert on the top of his head and straightened his hat.

"Maybe some food," Robert called over this shoulder as Chloe stepped away.

"Chopitos. That's what you need," Chloe said.

"Am I going to like that?"

"Tiny fried cuttlefish. You'll love it."

The last time Robert had had too much to drink had been at Debbie's college graduation dinner. But that wasn't like this. He'd had a couple of beers at the ballpark, but that was over an entire game. He tried to count the number of sangrias he had consumed. *Six?* It was likely more. *Over what, four hours? They went down so easy. The people were so nice. Is this what Spain is about?*

The cortado was served in a clear glass.

"There you go," Chloe said.

Robert lifted the glass for a closer look—the caramel-color below and the white ring at the top, like the head on a beer. "This is beautiful," he said.

"It is. No sugar?"

"No sugar."

"Chopitos will be out shortly," Chloe said. "I can always get you another coffee when you're ready."

Robert took a sip. He nodded.

"Glad you like it," she said.

Robert lifted his eyes to the dark sky.

"Do people, I don't know, do they live like this all the time?"

"Of course. That's all we do here. Drink and eat. Haven't you figured that out yet?"

Robert surveyed the plaza, and waved his free hand toward the many tables, the bottles of wine and the fiddler. "It's like there's not a care in the world," he said.

"Plenty of cares in the world, Robert."

"But you wouldn't know it."

Chloe surveyed the plaza. "There is a level of unfiltered joy here. Part of the culture. But we all have stuff to wrestle with. In Spain or not," she said.

"It's refreshing to see this."

"I'm certain it's one reason I stay."

"I believe that."

"There's space here to just *be*, I guess you could say."

Robert was curious about what she meant but he hesitated to respond.

"It's so cliché to say, really, but Spain is passionate about life. It was what I needed when I came here, in a lot of ways," Chloe continued.

"We all need a little of that."

"Some more than others," Chloe said.

Robert thought for a moment. *Am I happy?* It was an inquiry that arose from somewhere uncertain, somewhere in the spirit of the night. He surprised himself by asking it and he wasn't sure what it meant, but there it was.

Chloe paused to take in the fiddler's song. "Oh, I like this," she said, recognizing a melody. "He's played it many times here." She closed her eyes and swayed her hips, her lips slightly open as if she was about to say something but thought again.

"You're happy here, aren't you?" Robert asked.

"It's gypsy music. Always has this sort of happy longing."

Robert's wine buzz was beginning to wane, time and coffee doing its slow work. But for a moment he wished differently. Chloe, the music, the night—it all seemed made for a level of happy intoxication, a kind of mild abandon.

Chloe stopped swaying and opened her eyes. "I should check on your chopitos," she said. She touched Robert's arm and turned toward the kitchen entrance.

"You didn't answer my question," Robert said, surprising himself with his forwardness.

As Chloe rushed away, she waved a hand above her head, twisting it Flamenco style. "Of course, I am happy. I'm in Spain!" She turned to Robert. "I had none of this in America. None of it," she said. "Spain is my lover now. How do you like that for an answer?"

Chloe laughed, turned, and disappeared through the kitchen doorway.

As the fiddler continued to play, Robert lifted his eyes toward the church and its illuminated steeple and thought of Emma, how she would have liked Chloe, and how Chloe would have liked her. His marriage, he always believed was on the most solid ground, stable and full. He had never known another love. Emma was Robert's world and he missed her here in the plaza, under the soft light, with the fiddler now timidly bowing to a smattering of hand claps from the mildly drunk, the tired, the lonely, the wishful.

Before finishing his second cortado and paying the bill, Robert and Chloe agreed to tour the Alhambra together. She had been there many times, had an in on passes whenever she wanted. They were given to her for volunteering in the gardens last summer. She knew her way around the vast grounds, and assured Robert she could navigate the visit with ease. Chloe had the day off and Alhambra was on Robert's list of places to see.

They would meet in the plaza at the bus stop in late morning.

* * *

Robert and Chloe stood next to the signpost marking the arrival times for the bus.

"It's a short ride. Fifteen minutes, maybe," Chloe said. "We can take it home, too."

"They come every few minutes," Robert said, observing the sign.

"Transport is good in Spain," Chloe said.

"I want to get down to the sea, over to Seville, and maybe to the mountains on the east."

"You'll love Seville. Go to Rhonda, too. Amazing."

"I hear," Robert said. "I'll plan on it."

A trio of moped riders zipped by. Robert's eyes followed until they were over the hill and out of sight.

"You ever ride?" Chloe asked.

"Me? Oh, no. I had a friend with a motorcycle in high school. Closest I ever got. They always scared me."

"I used to own one. Boyfriend and I had cycles. We'd ride on the weekend together. Did it for a while. Long time ago."

A boyfriend? Robert thought. "And the scooters here? Do you ride them here?" he asked.

"I don't have one here. Someday, maybe. They're convenient. Easy to ride. They'd be fun along the coast when you get down there."

Robert laughed.

"Seriously. You can rent them," Chloe said.

"We'll see," Robert said.

"If you go east though, maybe not. Not for a first timer."

"No faith," Robert joked.

"I have plenty of faith, Robert. It's the mountain roads."

"Treacherous?"

"Up and down, around. You want to spend the time looking at the beauty. Not navigating a scooter."

"You're talking about Sierra Nevada, right?"

"Yeah, like America."

"The Spanish did a lot of conquering, didn't they?"

"They had their time. And when you're there in the mountains, do not miss the Indalo."

"That's a town?"

"It's a god. Well, it's not really a god, but it's an ancient symbol of the Messenger of the Gods. It's a carving in a cave outside Almeria."

"Cave drawings."

"He's good luck. There's a legend. The Indalo was a ghost that carried a rainbow in his hands."

"Where is it again?"

"In Almeria. Las Velez mountain range, actually. Same place Clint Eastwood filmed a bunch of those spaghetti westerns. Although, never understood why they called the ones filmed in Spain, spaghetti."

"I used to watch those late at night."

"The Indalo symbol is all over the area there, but you must see the carving. It's thousands of years old."

"And it'll bring me luck?"

Chloe looked beyond Robert over his shoulder. "The bus is here," she said.

Robert saw a stubby yet tall red vehicle turn the narrow corner near the old church. They climbed the short steps of the bus, and Chloe spoke to the driver, a few words of Spanish that Robert could not understand, and dropped coins in the tall metal container attached to the dashboard.

"My treat," Chloe said.

"Gracias," Robert said. "Es . . . ah estuvo . . . bien."

"Well, aren't we getting into the swing of things," Chloe said.

"Did I get that right?" Robert sighed.

"Not bad. Not bad at all."

There were two other people on the bus—a young woman in a purple dress holding a leather briefcase in her lap, watching the road out the window, and an old man in a straw fedora, a black cane resting on his knee. He sat in a middle seat.

"Hola," Robert said, tipping his hat.

The man nodded, and it was in that moment, in that simple exchange, that Robert found Granada. He couldn't explain it completely. He knew he was still the outsider, the American in a distant land far from home, but there was a shift on that bus, a kind of awakening in the late morning on the drive to Alhambra.

6

Robert had become accustomed to slow breakfasts of fruit, ham, eggs, slices of fresh tomato, bread, an espresso and then another. And like the last several mornings, he sat again in the small nook near the front of the hotel and read *The New York Times*, brought to the hotel one day beyond the publication date. This was not the paper he had grown up on, the one he'd read almost exclusively, the *Post-Gazette*. But he knew he wasn't going to get that in Granada. Books lined the shelves near the window, some in Spanish and others in English. There was a copy of *Don Quixote* and several Hemingway books, including *The Sun Also Rises*. Robert smiled when he saw it. There was Pablo Neruda and two books of poems by Federico Garcia Lorca. Robert opened one, curious that he had remembered Lorca's name from somewhere, but couldn't remember where. The volume was in the original Spanish. He had picked up more words and phrases over the last days, but reading Spanish was above his abilities. Still, despite this, Robert had come to enjoy his mornings, the gentle wake-up to the world alone in the nook with coffee, the books, the day-old news, and the comfortable old chair at the window.

Robert was to meet Chloe in an hour. She would come to the hotel. They would head for Sacromonte to see flamenco dancing. It's best to go at night, she told him, but that might be a bit overwhelming. There are usually crowds and a lot of drinking. There was dancing during the day for tourists. If he liked it, they could go back sometime for "the real party." Plus, she said, during the day, you can get an honest look at the way people lived there, the centuries of cave dwellers.

Robert was tasting the last of his coffee when the phone buzzed. The screen read *United States*.

"Hello.".

"Dad? Are you all right?"

"Honey. Hello. Your name didn't come up on the screen. Why did that happen?"

"You're safe, right? Where are you?"

"Done with breakfast. Reading. It's a beautiful day."

"That's good. That's good."

"Isn't it, like, the middle of the night at home?" Robert asked.

"Yeah. Bad dream. You were in it. Bad. Bad.

"Oh, honey. Nothing to be worried about. It's all good here."

Debbie sighed.

"I'm sorry about your dream," Robert continued.

"It was awful. And you're sure you're good, right?"

"Yes, all fine. Going to the caves today. Flamenco."

"That sounds very Spanish."

"It's Spain, honey."

"You're going by yourself?"
"Chloe."
"Who?"
"Chloe. I've told you about her, right?"
"Is that the waitress?"
"We've become friends."
"Dad. Be careful about this."
"She's so nice."
"Is she asking for money?"
"Honey. Of course not. No."
"I worry."
"An old man can't have a friend?"
"Send me a photo on your phone."
"Of Chloe?"
"Please. Send one."
"Well, I'm not sure . . ."
"At least take one, at least. If you remember."
Robert paused.
"Dad?" Debbie asked.
"How do I do that again? Send? I know how to take it. But send it?"
"Never mind. It's okay. What's her last name?"
Robert thought for moment. "I don't know her last name. That's funny, isn't it?"
"Please find out, okay?"
"Are you mad at me?"
"Dad, you're in another country. A million miles away. You're spending lots of time with someone you don't know. You're by yourself. You're old. All this is . . . I'm sorry. It's a lot."

"Honey. Honey. It's okay. You know, I used to have startling dreams sometimes. People drowning. Fires. Terrible stuff. Your mother would rub my arm to soothe me back to sleep."

"Find out her full name, this Chloe."

"I think you'd like her."

Debbie was silent.

"So, tell me about you," Robert continued. "What's happening there?"

The weather had been humid in Pittsburgh, she said. Work was work. Pirates had won a series against the Cardinals. The Cathedral of Learning on the Pitt campus was being renovated, a planned five-year job. Debbie had known how much her father had admired the Gothic Revival building, how it stood tall in the sky in the Oakland neighborhood. So, there was that. And she took a drive up to Seven Springs last Saturday with a friend.

Robert told her about the Alhambra, the mini-Morocco in Granada, the tasty tapas, but stayed away from mentioning Chloe again.

"And there was this odd moment in the cathedral here a few days ago," Robert said.

"What kind of moment?"

Robert caught himself. He shouldn't have brought it up. It would only worry Debbie more. But there it was.

"This young sister, this nun, she asked me if I was searching for something."

"What do you mean *searching*? Did you lose something. The key to the hotel? Are you forgetting things, again, Dad?"

"No, no. I'm pretty aware. It's funny. Different here, maybe. But no, I'm not forgetting."

Robert filled in the details of story at the church and the nun, deleting the parts that had made him uneasy, as a way to soften the story for Debbie.

"She seemed to know that I was, you know, sort of looking for, what was next, some kind of new chapter in my life. Kind of makes sense. Right?"

"Don't you find that strange?"

"It was sort of comforting," he said, lying a little.

"Uh-huh."

"The cathedral, by the way, is magnificent. I can send you photos."

"Dad, you don't know how to send? We went over this."

"Well, you can see them when I get home."

"You'll show me a photo of that woman, first."

* * *

Along the Paseo de lo Tristes, Robert sensed something familiar.

Robert and Chloe walked on the cobblestone path near the Darro. She lifted her face to the sky.

"Saffron," she said.

"Yes, that's it," Robert said. "Bought some a few days ago."

Ahead on the walkway was a spice dealer. Small wicker-like containers of loose spices lined a tiered wooden table.

"This is like in the Morocco section," Robert said. "And what is that sweet scent I'm getting now?" he asked turning toward the opposite side of the street.

"You're only catching that now? Today?" Chloe said. "It's the true scent of Granada, many would say."

"Flowers?"

"Wisteria," Chloe said.

"Gorgeous."

"It's everywhere."

Chloe pointed to an archway near a restaurant patio ahead where the flower draped from above a sky of velvet.

They sat for tapas and drinks at Afrazan. Beside them and across the river, the Alhambra rose above on the foothills. A canopy kept the sun off their backs.

"I didn't know there were places in the world like this," Robert said, taking his seat and surveying the view.

"There's so much we never experience," Chloe said, looking toward the river.

"They used to pan for gold in that water."

"Recently?"

"Ancient times. Romans."

"Paseo, that's patio or promenade, right? Tri . . . tris . . .te?"

"It's called the Promenade of the Sad."

"The sad?"

"Funeral processions used to come through this area on the way to the cemetery at the Alhambra."

"My goodness," Robert said. "My mind is spinning. All this history, food, smells. Can't take it all in."

"And sexy dancers," Chloe smiled.

"That, too," Robert said. "Should be interesting."

Chloe ordered two glasses of sangria. The waiter placed a small plate of prawns with olive oil and garlic, and another of ensaladilla rusa.

"I'm not sure how anyone smells anything anymore," Chloe said, her eyes returning to the wisteria.

"What do you mean?" Robert asked, lifting the glass to his mouth.

"The air. Even with those wonderful scents. It's filthy."

"Here?" Robert asked, looking to the sky.

"Spain is as bad as L.A. Madrid is worse. Even here, yes, even in Granada."

"My hometown used to be a dirty mess. Years ago, people who worked in the city brought an extra white shirt because the first would be full of soot before the end of the day."

"The hot weather here in the south especially doesn't help. Spain is not doing enough. There's a ministry for ecology in Spain. But it's the government. They don't know what they're doing."

Robert tasted a prawn.

"This spot has wonderful food," Chloe said. "Better than Lara."

Robert forked the ensaladilla. "Lots of garlic. How can you go wrong?" he said.

"Eat well now. Humans are going to kill us all," Chloe said, sipping her sangria.

Robert didn't want to talk about the world going to hell. Not here, not now. But it was impossible not to see Chloe's passion, albeit a glimpse. It was a likable trait. Debbie had her passions, too. The commitment she had made to buying her vegetables from the farm near Hickory, a way to support the locals. The crops were organic. Cost more. But it was important, she insisted. And that's what Robert saw in Chloe. He saw how important this was to her. But in moments, the other Chloe returned, the gracious one, the one showing Robert Spain, the one enjoying seeing him discover the beauty of her adopted country, the Chloe who smiled as she carefully searched the plate of prawns to spoon out a cut of garlic.

"I don't know what they do to these, but they are so lovely," Chloe said.

Robert watched her cut a prawn and take a small bite.

"You do that like a European," Robert said.

"What?"

"The knife, the fork. You cut it and keep the fork in your left hand."

"You mean this?" Chloe forked the remaining piece of prawn and lifted it to her mouth.

"Americans switch hands. And you're American."

"I've been here awhile."

"I guess that's fair."

"It's more efficient, don't you think? All that putting down the knife, moving the fork. Seems pointless."

"We shift to what's the custom, I guess. We adapt. In time, we adapt."

Chloe tasted the prawn. "I didn't eat much of these before here. Never had this before Spain or this either," she said, nodding toward the ensaladilla.

"You think you're a different person here?"

"How?"

"Being in Spain. You're Spanish now, in a way. Not American."

"How could I not be, to some extent. Spanish, that is. It has changed me," she said, raising her sangria glass.

"It must," Robert said.

"We become who we have to be," Chloe said.

Robert thought about Emma, and how he had decided to become something different because he simply had to.

"Like my hair," Chloe continued.

"What do you mean?"

"It wasn't always like this, like a boy."

"I had more hair once, too," Robert laughed, and tapped the top of his head.

"You know Emmylou Harris, the singer?"

"Sure."

"The young Emmylou. That was me."

"No."

"All the way to the middle of my back. Parted in the middle. Jet black. Straight as could be."

Robert imagined for a moment, the silkiness of it, how it would have floated over her shoulders and down across her chest. He thought of an Emmylou Harris song, the one about losing a love, pretending someone once loved you.

"From here to here," Chloe said, twisting in her chair to use her hand to mark a spot near her waist and then one near her left ear lobe.

"Just one day. Snip, snip," Robert said.

Chloe looked away toward the river. "Snip, snip."

"Was it the weather? So hot here."

"Something like that," Chloe said.

Chloe lifted her eyes toward the hills and what could be seen of the Alhambra. After a moment, her attention returned to the table and Robert's glass of ice and wine-soaked fruit. "You want another?" she asked.

With the sangria came more tapas, and an espresso and a small bit of chocolate at the end. And as they boarded the small bus that would climb the hills to Sacromonte and the caves and the entrance to Venta El Gallo, Robert noticed for the first time, a small tattoo on the nape of Chloe's neck below her hairline and above the top of her backbone, a tree in simple black ink, about two inches tall, wispy, and whimsical.

"Was that a change that came in Spain, too?"

"What's that?"

"The tree. On your neck."

Chloe paused. Thought for a moment. "Another life," she said. "Another time."

They took a double seat near the front, Robert at the window. Chloe wanted Robert to see the beauty of the short journey along the narrow roads that would climb to the ancient caves and archways on the slopes where hundreds of years before the gypsies escaped the walls of the old city and the Spanish Inquisition to find sanctuary.

Chloe and Robert were quiet now—the sangria, the sway and chug of the bus had left them with nothing more to say.

7

Someone had said once that the early morning sun in the south of Spain is a heavenly light. Chloe was thinking this as she stood near the window of her small apartment, coffee brewing in a moka pot at the stove. It had been a late night. She had expected to sleep longer, missing the agile rays of sun dancing through the glass and onto the hardwood floor. But there she was. And there they were, those rays, that heavenly light. She could not remember who said that about Spain's early hours. It didn't matter, what did was that it was there—the light, shining.

The flamenco dancing had been as it always was—passionate, vibrant, full of life. Chloe had been happy to see Robert take to it all—the wine and singing. They stayed longer than she had thought they might, but it was good and joyful. After a cab back to the Plaza de San Miguel, they sat in the light of the church and drank more wine, ate toasted bread, and talked of Spain's slow and celebratory days. Robert was now in Spain's embrace. He was a tourist, he knew, but he had told Chloe that he had sensed a shift, his heart beating differently. Chloe smiled. She had found herself drawn to the easy friendship, this stranger, this older man. Safe, she thought, and accepting the newness of Spain, his heart open. Safe was what she needed.

Chloe's window looked out to the hills toward the center of Granada. She was lucky to find this place—tiny but comfortable. The scene before her was more than she could have believed possible on her finances. She had had several homes, had moved often, and she knew it would soon be time to move again. And so, she lingered now, trying to take in the view from the window as much as she could, to remember. She had done the same late at night and in the middle of the day, lingered to remember.

Her first city after leaving America was Marrakesh. Tangiers after that. She moved to a farmhouse in Belgium for a time where the rent was free as long as she cared for the chickens. Southwest Ireland, near the coast came in the time before Spain. It was not easy, this moving, facing customs agents at each stop. But she had several passports, and she had learned to navigate the risks, to say the right things, to move in the world unnoticed. She was good at it. If you had the right frame of mind, she always told herself, then everything would be all right. What never was easy was the act of disappearing, how no one back home could ever matter again, how falling in love could never be, how making a friend could only be temporary. And although slipping through the shadowy corners of the world had become her life, Spain had taken hold like no other. Still, she had grown tired. After all the running, her heart was out of breath, and now her body, too, was failing.

It started with weakness in her right arm, her left leg, a twitching in her shoulder. She had fallen while working, an unexplained clumsiness she had not experienced before. Going before a doctor was too risky. But one morning, she found herself struggling to get out of bed. Standing and walking were nearly impossible. In a few hours, she was better, the tingling went away, only to return a week later and again after that. One morning, her hands had become numb, and alarm overtook fear and she found herself in the emergency room at the hospital. Tests were done. In days she knew what she had begun to suspect. "My father suffered the same," she told the physician. It was clear what was ahead for her, her body, her mind, her voice. For weeks Chloe considered giving in to the chase, to everything. The court would be merciful, she thought. There would be care in prison. *I could stop running.* But she knew, turning herself in was not an option. It was against all she believed, giving in to what she had vehemently rejected for so long. Maybe she could take on yet another identity, become someone important in the community, return to America and reinvent a secret life of doing good. Abbie Hoffman had done it. Living as a fugitive, he created an entirely new world for himself, new name—Barry Freed—living in the tiny town of Fineview, New York, working to save the St. Lawrence River from the environmental disaster of winter shipping. He testified before Congress as Barry. He fooled people for years. But this was a fantasy. It couldn't be. She was not Hoffman. She did not possess the same tenacity, the middle-finger sensibility that drove him. And beyond that, the violence and the deaths still haunted her. She hated herself for going along with what had happened that night in Oregon, for not speaking up, for standing before the fire and doing nothing, watching the night burn. The morning after the lumber company building in the mountains east of Eugene had turned to blackened wood and smoke, after two men had died inside, Chloe could not stop crying. She had been right there with the others, standing beside her fellow believers, her friends, the people she trusted, and she had watched as one of them threw a burning can of gasoline against the window, shattering it, the rooms inside quickly turning orange in the darkness. And now, as the early sun of a Granada morning flickered on her windowpane, it reminded her again of those flames. Chloe pressed her palms to the glass, as if reaching for something beyond what her eyes could see.

8

Emma would take her tea in the early morning on the stoop in front of the house and listen to the birds and watch the squirrels scamper at the base of a maple at the street corner. Sometimes it would be early enough to say hello to the milkman when there still were milkmen. Robert sat alone in the square, a short climb from his hotel through the narrow streets, thinking of her and those mornings.

The small modern café—the only place open—served espresso. Surrounding it were the whitewashed outside walls of tapas restaurants and a few empty tables among the trees. And at the edge of the square, vendors assembled wooden stands and two small white tents. Baskets of fruit and bread sat in the bed of a red truck. It was market day here in the square. Emma would have loved this, Robert thought.

There was still music in Robert's head. The guitars of flamenco, and the slap and clatter of castanets. Emma might not have wanted to stay as long as Robert and Chloe had. Too much stimulus for too long a time. But she would have appreciated it. The colors and the life-affirming sounds of six-strings echoing in the caves would have delighted her. And now, in the square, comfortably weary from the night before, Emma was with Robert. Not that he didn't always think o her, but in the already warming first hours of light, after a joyful night, Robert longed for Emma be with him, holding his hand, welcoming another day. He often thought of her hands, her slender fingers, the softness of her palms, her nails painted a delicate lavender, the ring she never removed, even when she washed dishes or put her hands in the dirt of the small garden to plant marigolds at the front of their home.

Robert wondered, again, as he had before if Emma would have liked Chloe. It had surprised him, how he had taken to this fast acquaintance. Robert knew little about Chloe, still he was spending time with her, allowing her to show him Granada, eating and drinking with her. *Maybe Debbie was right?* The analysis, the overthinking of how and why he moved through those days back home after Emma was something he wanted to end. His life had always been analytical, making the right choices at the right times. It was what one does when building a life, having a child, building a home, keeping a job. But he no longer wanted to live like that. Robert hoped he could find a way to simply *be*. He didn't know what that meant in everyday terms, in this new chapter of a life, or what that looked like now. But he was trying in his own way and maybe Chloe was helping, maybe she was part of the change. And maybe, Emma would have understood.

"Hola. Cuanto?" Robert asked.

The woman was dressed in white, wearing a colorful silk neck scarf. She arranged avocados on a long table.

"Cincuenta por uno," she said.

Robert counted out some change and handed the coins to the woman.

"Naranja, tambien?" the woman asked.

Robert was unsure of the question but understood when the woman held up an orange.

"Si," he said. "Cincuenta?"

The woman placed the avocado and the orange in a small brown bag and handed it to Robert.

"Buenos dias, señor," she said.

"No, no. I must pay you for all of it," Robert insisted.

"La naranja es mi regalo."

Uncertain, Robert could only smile.

"A gift," the woman said in English, hoping she had the right intonation.

"Gracias," Robert said. "Thank you, señora."

Robert peeled the orange to separate the wedges, eating each one slowly and tasting the bright sweetness. He used his thumb nail to stripe a line across the avocado and peel away part of the skin, revealing the green and yellow flesh. It was firm and a bit unripe but offered the taste of nuts and cream. Robert ordered another espresso, and after attempting several times to catch the eyes of the woman who now carried a small wooden crate of lemons from the truck bed to the table, he called out.

"Señora!"

She lifted her head as she snatched the yellow fruit, two at a time from the crate.

"Muy Bueno," Robert said.

"Estoy feliz," said the woman.

Feliz. That means happy. Like Feliz Navidad.

It was then that Robert remembered. *I haven't taken an antacid in days. How about that?* Robert was certain that Emma was watching from somewhere, now assured that he was getting along.

In a few days, Robert would head south to the mountains. Chloe made the trip once a year, a pilgrimage to Almeria and Sierra de Maria-Los Velez National Park to reset her balance. That's what she called it. She had asked Robert if he'd like to come along, warning him that it is dry and rocky and hot, but that there also were glorious peaks and the deep green of pines. You might see a peregrine falcon soaring above us, she said. And of course, there is Indalo Man.

It was another chance to step out of what Robert had been.

Before leaving the square, Robert made his way around the far side of the small market, drawn in by a sweet, yeasty scent. A vendor had placed dozens of loafs of pan de Alfacar on a wooden table, a spongy bread made with spring water found outside Granada.

"May I?" Robert asked, reaching for a small sample arranged on a plate.

The man nodded from behind the table.

"Deliciosa," he whispered, kissing his fingertips. The man continued in broken English.

"Señor, you are tasting Spain."

With a fresh loaf under his arm and a small bottle of olive oil he had also purchased at the market, Robert walked to the Plaza de San Nicolas where from a seat on the stone wall and a distant view of the Alhambra, he pulled away pieces of bread and soaked each with silky oil, tasting something both exotic and familiar, a bit of what was and what could be.

9

It was midafternoon and Debbie had taken a late lunch. She sat on the bench at the small picnic table in the park near her office with a deli sandwich and an iced tea from the shop in the strip mall up the road. She had made a couple of phone calls over the last two days. One never connected. Another did, but Robert had not answered. She left a voice message, but she assumed her father probably wouldn't know how to retrieve it. It frustrated her but she was over it. *It was the trip of a lifetime*, she now reminded herself. *Dad had been okay when we talked.* She was also better about the companion. *Maybe it's all right. Maybe it's good. Maybe, if she's a decent person, she's keeping an eye on him.* Still, Debbie was Robert's daughter, and he was her father.

She dialed. After a few fast rings, Robert answered.

Despite the early hour in Spain, Robert's voice was bright and alive. Debbie told herself not to probe so much this time, not as she had done before, asking only about the weather and what kind of food he'd been eating. Nothing about the waitress. Not a word about the worries that remained. Her father was full of things to say, and he said them with the excitement of a young man on an adventure. Debbie thought she could sense his heart beating thousands of miles away. The phone call reminded her of Christmas mornings, the ones she had remembered as a girl, Dad singing "Jingle Bells" as he made pancakes, laughing as he watched her tear away the wrappings around a big new stuffed animal, a friendly lion with a fluffy mane. It had been a long time since she had heard her father like this. Alert. Alive. He spoke of the coming drive south with Chloe, the chance to see the sea, the mountains, the caves, and a drawing on a wall called Rainbow Man. Throughout the call, Debbie held on to what she had promised herself and found a way to allow her father to be happy.

Afterward, Debbie Googled on her phone the words *Rainbow Man* and *parks in southern Spain* and *summer weather conditions* in the Spanish mountains. She read the stories, the legends, and the posts of the travel blog of an amateur adventurer who had made her way to the caves. The blogger had posted photos of the carvings and she wrote of how seeing them had given her peace and a sense of wonder. That's what Debbie hoped now for her father. Worrying would be there, always, but maybe, she thought, she could forget this for a little while.

On the drive home that evening, Debbie detoured to her father's house to pick up the newspapers and his mail. In between a Giant Eagle flyer and a Bass Pro Shop catalog was a notice from Western Pennsylvania Gas and Electric. Robert had seven days to pay what he owed, or the utilities would be shut off.

He had forgotten to pay his bill. Debbie could only smile.

10

Each time Chloe had made the trip, Chloe had borrowed a car. Renting a vehicle was problematic. She needed identification and a credit card, both of which she avoided having to show or use.

"What is this?" Robert asked as he eyed the vehicle from the passenger side and Chloe placed his small brown luggage bag in the backseat.

"A Polo. I think that's what they call it," Chloe said.

"Oh, it's a Volkswagen," Robert said, noticing the emblem below the hood.

"Don't think you have this particular one in America. Good gas mileage. Serves the purpose," Chloe said.

"Carbon footprint, right? And how far are we going again?"

The plan was to travel from Granada to the southern coast near Almeria and then northeast to the Vélez Blanco to the park and the caves, staying overnight in the area before heading back. Robert had read about Spain's southern coast, and thought maybe before the pilgrimage to Rainbow Man, she could show him Spain's beaches. Chloe agreed even though the destinations were a distance apart, a two-hour detour. Still, it had been some time since she had been to the coast. The trips to the mountains and to Rainbow Man had always been made with singular focus. But now she had a companion. She secured two days off from the restaurant, and her friend had offered the car for as long as she needed it. It would be 170 kilometers to the coast and about 170 more north to Sierra de María-Los Vélez Natural Park, mostly on good roads.

The drive south along the edge of the Sierra Nevada mountains toward Motril on the coast moved through grove after grove of olive trees, craggy and deep-rooted, up and down and over the rolling hills of dusty ground in hues of burnt orange and muted red. As Robert and Chloe neared the coast, low mountains rose from the desert ground. Outside Motril, the terrain turned lush. The beaches flat and filled with swimmers. The road traveled close to the sea and as it turned east, Robert could see the bodies and the surf. When he lowered his window, a gust assaulted him. This was the legendary coastal wind. It was always windy in Motril, Chloe told him. The waters filled with jellyfish, Chloe said. She had taken on the role of a tour guide while Robert asked questions, his eyes on the beauty before him.

The road skimmed the rocky coast of the Alboran Sea. Moving east, the beaches became more remote. From the road and below the cliffs, Robert could see coves and pebbled sand with no one there, not a soul, as if he alone was discovering a secret. The sunlight touched the soft waves, splashing the beach in silence. From Motril to Castrell de Ferro, some 25 kilometers, hardly a word was exchanged between he and

Chloe. What Robert was witnessing had seized his voice until he could no longer remain quiet.

"It makes you remember how wonderful it is to be alive," Robert said, his eyes on the sea.

Chloe watched the road through the windshield, smiling only when she sensed Robert turning from his view to look at her. "You could say that," she said.

"Can't everyone say that?" Robert asked.

He turned back to the window.

"Why are you here?" Robert asked.

"Here? In the car? With you?"

"Well, yeah," Robert grinned. "But really, why are you living in this place and not somewhere else? I know you said you love it. You clearly do. But why did you choose to be here? You have family."

"I've been a lot of places," Chloe said.

"But why here, why now?" Robert asked, looking now directly at Chloe.

Chloe shrugged. "You tell me," she said, offering her hand to the scenery. "It's pretty nice."

"Just curious," Robert said, returning his eyes to the passenger window.

Only the churn of the car and the whir of wind could be heard now. Robert wanted to ask more questions, but he didn't, believing he might be intruding, his curiosity moving beyond the appropriate space new friends place between one another.

After several minutes, Chloe spoke.

"Yes. I do have family in America," she said, her eyes remaining on the road.

"But I have left that behind."

"It happens," Robert said.

"It's complicated."

"I don't want to pry."

Chloe shook her head. "It's not that. I just don't talk about any of this. It's thousands of miles away. It's a lifetime ago."

"We can change the subject," Robert said.

Chloe leaned back in her seat and regripped the steering wheel. "I've been doing that for years, changing the subject."

The road hugged the coast as they rode above La Mamola, an ancient fishing village. White buildings lined the beach and jetties stretched out to the sea. The air smelled different, saltier, and sunlight glinted off gentle waves. Sandy beaches fell into giant rock formations.

Robert leaned out the window, hoping to see more clearly.

"We can stop," Chloe said.

"It looks magnificent."

"You like fish, right?"

"Some true ocean fish, I don't know."

"Best octopus in Spain."

"Never had it."

"Grilled. Luscious. And La Mamola is the place."

Chloe turned the car at the next exit and made her way along Sanchez Moreno, the avenue at the beach's edge. Against the stonewall and benches opposite the restaurants and shops, merchants sold clothes, sandals, fruit, and breads. One merchant, an old woman sitting in a folding chair near a table filled with pomegranates, waved to acknowledge Robert's smile. He waved back. It was as if he had been given a gift.

Chloe pulled the car into a parking space, turned the key, and took a deep breath.

"She jumped from the Golden Gate Bridge."

"What?"

"My mother. She jumped."

Robert's face flushed.

"She survived. She was rescued. She told me years later that as she was falling—air rushing past, everything became very quiet—she knew she had made a mistake, she knew she wanted to live. She didn't want to die."

"I don't know what to say."

"It was a long time ago. She was young. Before her family moved to Georgia. It changed her in so many ways, as you can imagine. And then when I was a teenager, about the age when she jumped, she worried that I would do the same. Jump. Take pills. Cut my wrists. She was waiting for the day."

Robert turned in his seat to face Chloe more directly. His eyes became moist, his face flushed.

"There's a hell of a lot I've left behind in America," Chloe said.

Robert swallowed and turned his eyes to the windshield and a sidewalk of window-shopping tourists. "Did you ever? he asked.

"No yet," she said, smiling.

"Chloe?"

"Dark humor."

"I'd say so."

"There's a lot I want to forget," she said.

Chloe lifted her head high, stretching out her neck, and with purpose, to summon something new, she drummed the top of the dashboard.

"Enough of this. Let's get some octopus."

The table was draped in a white linen cloth and angled at the window that looked out to the sea. Red carnations burst from a black ceramic vase in the table's center. Chloe had ordered a bottle of Tempranillo from the Ronda region and it had been delivered and poured. But the beauty and civility of a Spanish afternoon meal in a seaside restaurant, could not erase what had been said. Like the bones of the men and women murdered along this coast during the Civil War more than a half-century ago, Chloe's words could never be erased from a memory simply by burying them. Spain's history of sorrow would always shape its people, and the desperation of Chloe's mother would always remain.

Robert raised his wine glass and offered a toast to life and the sea, and a safe trip north.

11

In the broad and open plaza, children played. Two young boys kicked a ball, dodging the palms as if the lofty trees were defenders in a football match, the slap and pop of the strikes echoing off the fortified cathedral walls. It was a hot and dry late afternoon in Almeria, but the boys dismissed the heat, playing in the sun with no evidence of fatigue. They spoke no words to one another, focusing only on the ball and its trajectory. And so, when Robert and Chloe stepped along the plaza toward the elaborate stone entrance, the boys continued without interruption as if alone in the world.

Robert wiped sweat from his forehead and lifted his eyes to the statue of the Virgin Mary, the Christ Child in her arms, above the massive wooden doors. He thought of his church back home, the marble statue of Mary at its doorway, and how Emma would touch it for good luck as she entered.

"It was a mosque before this," Chloe said.

"The Muslim invaders?" Robert asked. He had come to understand a bit of the history.

"See those tiny windows up high?" Chloe asked, pointing. "They put cannons up there. It was a fortress. The two sides of the soul of Spain. Christianity and war."

"We all have many sides, don't we?" After a moment, Robert added, "I feel overwhelmed standing before churches like this." He remembered the young nun he encountered in Granada in the first days of his visit, the one who asked if he had been searching.

"I haven't been in Almeria in some time. But when I've been, I've always come here," Chloe said.

"Brought up Catholic?"

"I was brought up nothing, I guess you would say."

"Then what is it? Why do you come?"

Chloe thought for a moment. "Just in case," she said.

Robert smiled.

"And each time I have a word with God inside."

"Just in case?"

"Just in case."

The weight of the church, its heavy imposition was unmistakable. Chloe felt it on her shoulders as she walked on marble tiles toward the altar of gold. Robert stood at the back of the cathedral, watching. Although its doors were open and tourists and worshippers were welcome, no one else was inside, the echoes of centuries the only occupants. Order and reverence commandeer one who comes to this medieval space, a requirement for the faithful and an obligation for all others. For Chloe, the burden of it only emboldened her, and at the altar she stood, her arms crossed at her waist, her eyes raised to the marble statues of the saints.

It's come to this, again, she prayed. *You and me, and my disbelief. If that's what it is. I'm never sure. Something has to be bigger than each of us, but I'm not certain it's you—God, Jesus, or whatever you are. Show me a sign, I say sometimes. And maybe you show me, but I miss it. Or maybe I'm waiting for something that will knock me over, wow me, like the best act of a magician. And then I think, maybe it's not in the big things. Maybe it's in the simple, quiet things that you prove yourself.*

Or maybe, forgive me, but maybe it's all bullshit. This is all manmade crap. Faith, they say, you must have it. The belief in something you can't prove. That never made any sense to me. But here I am, again, standing here, talking to you. And it's been a while. And I still don't know what it is I'm looking for.

So, what's new? I'm still running, hiding, but tired. You know all that. We've talked. And now, my nerves and my muscles will fail me in time and my heart will stop. I'll wither, to a helpless mess. It will be painful, I know. And who do I have to comfort me? Many would say I have you. But then I have to believe first, don't I?

So, what to do? Try to believe and find some contentment if that's possible anymore. And what is it that I'm doing, exactly? Trying to make myself believe to give myself comfort, to pretend somehow? That doesn't seem right.

I'm not afraid of dying. Not at all. I'm afraid of living this way. What good is that? Who does it serve? So, I have another idea. You won't like it and I'm not sure I should tell you, maybe not now. Certainly, if I did there would be wrath, as the Bible says. You would come down hard. And if you are who they say you are, again, well, you already know what I'm thinking, planning, considering. So, what difference does it make?

Why am I telling You all this if I don't believe? It's really simple. It's a fail-safe measure. That's what I've told my friend. I'm hedging my bets. That's a sorry way of dealing with this, isn't it? A sad and maybe even despicable way of dealing with our complicated relationship. But so human, wouldn't you agree?

I'm here not because I want help or some sign or expect some revelation. I'm here because I'm trying to save my own ass. And because I believe if you are who you are, you will forgive me. Forgive everything. Forgive mistakes. Forgive my disbelief. And even forgive what I will eventually do. So, God, get ready for me. If you're there, if you are real, I will be at the gate soon and I'll look in your eyes and beg for forgiveness. You are a benevolent God, right? That's what I hear.

This is where I am. And you must admit, I'm being honest here telling you this when I'm not sure you're even listening. So, Amen, God. Amen. And thanks, if you are real, for hearing me out.

Chloe turned and marched to the back of the cathedral where Robert stood. "Let

go," she said.

"Are you all right?" Robert asked.

"Done here. Need to go."

Chloe hurried past Robert and through the massive cathedral doors to the plaza. As the doors closed behind her, Robert noticed against the wall near the entrance, a marble vessel of holy water. He dipped his fingertips in and made the sign of the cross before stepping out into the late day sun.

* * *

Spain was crystalized in the color of white and raw sugar along the first leg of the drive north from Almeria. The arid land and the tumbling hills of stone stretched to the horizon, the paleness colliding with the blue sky. The Sierra de los Fibrales—the largest mountain range in southern Spain—was far to the northeast. At the highest peak—Calar Alto—was an observatory where one of Europe's largest telescopes captured the heavens. Along A-7 it was the land that ruled. Bleakness was stark beauty and emptiness an unexpected solace. It was only in Sorbas when patches of green scrub and small trees began to appear at the base of the hills.

"What if God doesn't really forgive us in the end," Chloe said, breaking a long silence.

"What if he simply corrects our mistakes, instead? Sets everything straight."

"You sure you're not a believer?" Robert asked.

"Someone said that time polishes the soul, it shines it up, and in time we see our true selves in the reflection."

"Others see who we really are before we do. Don't you think?"

"You see the real me and I see the real you?"

"And then maybe in time, we finally figure it out."

"Who we are?"

"Who we are," Robert said. He turned his eyes to the passenger window. "See what a few minutes in a Spanish cathedral on a hot late afternoon will do to you."

"Damn it, God. You're fuckin' with me."

Chloe and Robert laughed.

"A bit harsh," Robert said. "But yeah, He does that."

"He?"

"Okay. I'll give you that. *She*, maybe, does that."

Chloe reached to touch Robert's arm. "I'm happy you're here," she said.

* * *

Mojacar is whitewashed, an old Moorish town nestled in the hills above the sea. Here, they ate Moroccan food on a patio lit by tiny lights. They would spend the night at a small apartment where a rose bush grew along the shutters of the window at the entrance. Inside, twin beds—draped in bright orange spreads separated by an oak table that sat in the center of the room. A small green pot on the nightstand held a red geranium. Beside the flower was a well-read copy of *The Collected Poems of Federico Garcia Lorca*, a bilingual edition, the back cover stained by a spill of red wine. On the wall opposite the beds, a small stone carving of the Indalo.

"He is everywhere," Chloe said. "On building walls, storefronts, statues in the square."

"Mojacar has adopted him," Robert said.

"It's a bit commercialized at times. Jewelry and t-shirts. But that's what happens with symbols. Like those t-shirts of Che Guevara."

Robert nodded. He looks at the beds. "How are we doing this?" he asked

"You get one. I get one."

"Well, yes. Which one, though?"

Chloe sat on the edge of the bed nearest the door.

"This one's mine. You good?"

"Sure," Robert said. He opened his bag to find his toiletry case, waved his toothbrush, and turned to the washroom.

"Robert," Chloe said softly. "It's okay."

"It's a bit, I don't know, odd. No. That's not right. Not odd." Robert looked in the bathroom mirror. "I'm more than twenty years older than you and here we are."

"I think you know I don't bite."

"My daughter would not understand." Robert could see Chloe in the glass. He waved his toothbrush again. "I need to clean up."

Remaining on the bed's edge, waiting for her turn to prepare for the night, Chloe thumbed the book of poems. On one dogeared page, a familiar stanza from a poem she had read before: "Song of the Barren Orange Tree."

"Woodcutter," she read in a whisper. "Cut my shadow from me."

Chloe held the book to her chest, and before returning it to the bedside table, she straightened the dogeared page, smoothing it with her hand as if trying to erase what someone had wished to remember.

12

In the morning at the bathroom mirror, Chloe brushed her hair, pulling the black bristles close to her right temple. The gray in her hair was more noticeable now. She'd had first seen the color changes a year ago, and now there were more strands. She brushed behind her ears and at the forehead's hairline in slow, meticulous strokes. As she moved her hand and the brush toward the back of her head, she sensed numbness. It came first in her wrist and then her fingers, first tingling and then deadness. The brush slipped from her grasp. She massaged her dead hand with the other, hoping to bring it to life. This had happened before, most often when she would forget or reject her medicine, missing a day or two. The pills were inside her luggage in the other room and Robert, she believed, was still sleeping. She would take them later, she thought. It would be okay. She would manage for now. But as she reached for the fallen brush, there was the sensation of pins in her right leg below the knee. Chloe clutched the corner of the counter, but her trembling hand could not steady her. When she dropped to the floor, the brush fell too, clattering on the tile, shattering the morning's calm.

"All okay?" Robert asked from the bed.

He was not sleeping. Hadn't slept most of the night. When he would experience relative calm and contentment, his eyes closed and his mind quiet, he would soon be overwhelmed with uncertainty.

"Sorry . . . I'm . . ."

Robert moved to the edge of the bed, his feet on the floor. "You need some help?"

"No, no," Chloe said, her body on the cold tile, her right foot now quivering.

Robert sat quietly, listening. He sensed movement from behind the bathroom door, a mild groan, and another. He wanted to knock and insist he was available, but reserve got the best of him.

"If you need something," he said.

"It happens," Chloe said, struggle to return to the mirror.

"What happens?"

Chloe looked at her reflection—her face colorless. The numbness in her hand had subsided enough to use it to balance her body but her leg needed more time. She reached to massage her knee and shin.

"In my bag, on the side pocket, there are pills. They're in a small container."

Robert stood and surveyed the room. On a corner chair, he spotted Chloe's opened luggage. "You want me to go in your bag?"

"Side pocket."

The numbness would fade. Chloe knew this. But it would return soon if she didn't take the pills. The pills did not solve anything. They only prolonged the time between episodes.

Robert stood before the door with the pill box and tapped lightly with his knuckles.

"You can come in," Chloe said.

With his eyes downward, Robert turned the knob and through the opening, enough only for his hand, he offered the box. "Are you sure you're okay?" he asked.

"It's all right. I'll manage."

Without pushing, the door slowly opened on its own. Chloe, in a blue t-shirt and cotton shorts, her back against the counter to steady herself, could see Robert in his bed clothes.

"Robert," Chloe said, hoping to coax him to look directly at her.

Without lifting his head, Robert brought his eyes to Chloe.

Chloe took a pill from the box, placed it on her tongue, and swallowed. "I'm dying," she said. "And it's as simple as that."

* * *

The coffee was dark and the right kind of bitter. Robert had liked it that way before he came to Spain and found espresso. And now alone, at a table on the patio of a café, a short walk from the apartment, he had ordered what had once been familiar. After the bathroom and the pill, Chloe told him how things would go, the way her condition would progress, how she would lose control of her hands, her legs, how eventually she wouldn't be able to talk, and at the end, she would not be able to breath. All Robert could say was "I'm so sorry." And now while Chloe rested in bed, the medicine taking hold, her body finding temporary balance, Robert could only think of himself. Selfish. Shameful, he thought. But what does one do, how does one act after shared news like this? *We hardly know one another. Yet here we are on a trip together—traveling, eating, drinking, talking—and you tell me you're dying.*

It was a high school party where Robert and Emma had first met. She had noticed him standing on the front porch of a classmate's home on Fisher Street with several other boys. It was summer and the friend's parents had taken a long weekend in Deep Creek, Maryland where they had rented a small lake cottage for a few days. It was a perfect night for Beatles' record and cans of Iron City. When Emma first saw Robert, he had an Iron in his hand. She thought he was handsome in a preppy sort of way, his hair, long in front, swooping over his forehead like Jack Kennedy's did when he walked the beach. Robert wore khaki shorts and a short sleeve light blue colored shirt.

Emma was interested in photography and took pictures for the school newspaper. She was known to show up at football games, dances, and parties like this one with a camera in her hand. That evening she carried a Kodak Instamatic. She pointed the lens toward Robert and his friends, and as the bulb flashed, the boys turned toward it. "It's the camera girl," one of the boys said. Robert's eyes remained on Emma as she lowered the lens and returned a smiled. "The camera girl?" Robert asked.

The party progressed and Emma took several more photos of Robert. He had noticed each time she had snapped a shot, and by the fifth flash, he approached her. "Am I going to get a chance to see those sometime?" he asked. In time, he would. And in time, there would be more photos of Robert, and soon photos of the two of them together. Photos Emma would take with her camera and photos others would take. Photos at the prom. Photos at graduation. A photo of the two of them eating ice cream cones. A photo of them making faces at the camera as Robert pushed Emma on a park swing. Dozens of photos. There would be wedding photos taken by Robert's uncle to save money. But other photos the wedding day would be taken by Emma, the bride in her white dress, snapping photos inside the reception hall at the VFW in Mt. Oliver. She had remained the camera girl. In three large black photo albums on a shelf in the living room of Robert's home, hundreds of photos Emma had taken since the ones at the party where they had first met and throughout their lives together had been carefully arranged, labeled, and dated. There were holes in the continuum, years missed it seemed, but the collection was nothing less than a photographic document of their relationship. It had been a long time since Robert had opened any of those albums, couldn't find the will. But now on this morning at the café, he wished each had been right in front of him, in his hands, reminding him of all the life there had been before death, all the smiles before Emma would be gone. Maybe in those old photographs, he thought, there would be an answer, something to go on, showing him a way to face the news he had been given, how to navigate what had become a strange and awkward arrangement.

It would be a late start to what had been planned, but in time, Chloe would regain her steadiness, and they would begin the 117km drive north with Robert behind the wheel. Through rugged land to Cueva de los Letreros, they would travel and once there they would meet a guide, and hike to the site of the ancient stone drawings that had lured so many.

13

The stout houses of Velez Blanco—the color of sand and bleached stone—sat clustered on the hills below a 16th century Renaissance castle. One kilometer outside the village was the cave. Not a cave at all but a steep cliff wall underneath a natural overhang. There on the cliff, visible from the stone steps along the fenced-off trail below were the paintings, displayed as if ancient man had constructed a gallery.

A guide from the park stood near to assist in understanding, but Chloe knew where she was and why.

"There are many paintings, most in red. Probably made from iron deposits and some sort of paste," Chloe whispered.

Triangles, symbols for water, lightening, the sun, the moon, goats, and deer. Calcium deposits had muted some over the centuries. Weather had washed out others.

"Archeologists come to help restore them. I've seen it. Painstaking work," Chloe continued. After a pause, she pointed. "There he is."

The figure of a man, standing with his legs apart and his arms reaching up. He appeared to be holding a bow above his head, a rainbow many say.

"A symbol of unity," Robert said.

"He's a protector. The legend goes that if given an Indalo figure—jewelry or drawing—all evil spirits and bad things will be pushed away."

Robert eyes moved up and down the steep slope. Clearly, this must have been a place of ceremony, he thought. Rituals and sacrifices. It was where prehistoric man came to revere and pray to the land, to nature, to what the Earth had given them. Rainbow Man was likely a hunter, aiming his bow toward the sky, targeting a bird in flight. But that hunter may have been much more, he may have been the hero, the one who brought food and prolonged existence, the human god of abundance, a sustainer of life.

Robert turned to view the village below and the layer of sun-soaked haze now building along the mountain. Returning his eyes to the wall, he found Chloe, sitting cross-legged on the stone steps, her hands in her lap, cheeks stained by dusty tears.

Emma had cried like this, quietly inside, her eyes the only proof of her emotion. No sobs. No whimpers. Robert remembered silent tears as he stood at the altar on his wedding day, the silent tears at the funeral for Emma's mother at St. Basil's, and at Debbie's college graduation. There was crying at Sunday mass when the choir sang "Ave Maria." Tears in the movie theater at the end of *Dr. Zhivago*. Emma's tears came easily in sadness and in joy. But they were always hushed. For Robert, tears were infrequent. Deep inside is where Robert felt.

And he felt much. But outside, he was controlled, always believing he should be the one to keep it together.

"Are you all okay?"

"It's just so much to deal with," Chloe sighed.

Years ago, Robert had heard, maybe on one of the PBS shows he liked to watch on Saturday afternoons, that many studies had been conducted over the decades on why we cry. Scientists had definitively discerned that it was a remarkably human act. No other creatures cry. It was once believed, maybe in Medieval times, that crying was linked to the heart heating up in sorrow or happiness, the body creating vapor to cool it down, the tears being the manifestation of this physiological process. It was also once believed that crying helped to remove toxins from the body in times of stress. In time, researchers came to believe that tears were there to help us bond. We are born unequipped to rationalize emotions, humans never fully discovering how to age out of helplessness. Our crying signals to others that there is something going on in our life with which we have no ability to cope. Crying shows the rest of the human world that we are endlessly vulnerable, setting off empathy and compassion, a part of being uniquely alive. All of this made sense to Robert at that moment, but it didn't answer the question of why some of us cry more than others, why some are so hushed, and why he, like the men he knew, the men of his generation, had been destined to be seen as forever detached despite how the heart ached.

Robert reached to touch Chloe's shoulder and then thought differently. "Are these happy tears?" he asked. "They must be. This place. Here and now. Aren't they happy tears?"

Chloe closed her eyes and tilted her head to the sky. "Dying is always about *when,* isn't it? It's not a *never* question. We know that. It's *how* that's the mystery, the unknown for all of us. And that *when.*" She looked at the cave's wall and Rainbow Man. "How stupid to think he could save me."

"Maybe he wasn't meant to be a savior," Robert said. "Maybe he was meant to be a guide, you know? Like a guardian angel. Protection and unity, as the legend goes. But the unity thing is different, right? As in your own inner . . . what would be the word?" Robert thought for a moment. "Harmony. Inner harmony," he said.

Chloe wiped her cheeks and stood. "I know the *how*, Robert," she said.

"The *how?*"

"Known it for a long time now."

Robert squinted. Chloe took his hand.

"You're a good man, Robert. And I need you to help me. I hope you will understand."

On the two-hour drive back to Granada, Chloe removed the lid off each of her life's boxes, one by one, boxes she had kept on a shelf for a long time. There was the box about Oregon and the fire, the terribleness of it, the dead, the guilt. She opened the box about her name. It was Megan, not Chloe. Megan Wilkins. The fugitive box, the box about her running for years from country to country, faking her passport, dodging border patrols. And as the kilometers ticked off and the night fell, she opened the final box, the box holding her *how*, her plan, the one containing the drug she had secured, and how she was hoped Robert could be her confidant in what she believed was an act of mercy. The fast and untethered friendship, and the short history between them would make it simpler on them both, she insisted. As simple as anything like this could be. Chloe needed him; someone she could rely on to see her through it. They had built trust, but no emotional bond of family or lover to complicate things. Robert was not someone who would try to change her mind, she believed, not someone who would try to stop her. And the truth was, Chloe had no one else.

14

For the first time since his visit, Robert had noticed how many in Spain searched for and found shade. He wondered why he hadn't noted this before. It took a walk through the Parque de Maria Luisa in Seville for him to realize how Spaniards sought the sunless side of the walkway and street so they might last in the heat. The hat he had purchased when he first arrived was still with him, and it was a walk along the fence around the lotus pond where he fully understood the goodness of that hat in the relentlessness of the Spanish sun. A young couple held hands and maneuvered back and forth out of the bright light to the cooler shadows of the trees. They were a beautiful pair, this couple. And that was something else he had noticed more so in Seville than in Granada or anywhere else—how beautiful the people were; how it was hard to take your eyes off them. Earlier that day, there had been a wedding party at the vast Plaza de España, a photographer following close by. The bride in white lace, the gown's train held in her hand above the ground, her olive skin lustrous, her dark hair in ringlets along her cheeks. The groom—dark, slender, tall—a red rose attached to his black lapel, smiled in the glory of her. Maybe it was Seville, the grand plaza and the park, the light and the shade that had refocused how Robert was now viewing this country and its people. He had come to Seville to be alone, to think, and although that is what he had been doing, he also had permitted himself to discover something more here, something revealing. Much had changed now, the magnificence of a life more apparent. Robert had sought the shadows, but he also had stood in the sun.

Seville was a detour, an unexpected addition to the original trip. It came after what Chloe had asked of him. When he called Debbie to tell her he was staying longer, there was surprised silence and then many questions. Do you have the money? Where are staying now? Is it that woman? Robert answered as best he could without revealing the anxiety that had built inside, and without lying. This involved the skill of evasion, a hard task for Robert. He wasn't so sure he had convinced Debbie that his decision to remain came simply from the joy of his travels.

Part of Robert was angry. *What a burden to place on me? Chloe had thought this through, and believed in it, but to ask me to be a partner in it is unfair.* He was a stranger to her. Still, there were moments when he found himself understanding. Maybe he was the best one to help, the best one to support her. Maybe a stranger is what was needed. Someone with less connective emotional tissue. The request would test him, force him to disregard his faith, not to mention the lawlessness of it. *Could I be charged, tried, maybe imprisoned?* If he physically assisted—administered a drug or encouraged Chloe to take her life—it might be a crime. Yet, if he only stood by, if he only failed to stop her, and if she had stated her wish in a document, signed and clear, and he had only allowed that wish to come true, the act might be within reason. Yes, Robert was angry. But maybe more with himself.

At the Gorieta de la Concha, Robert sat on a tiled bench of blue and copper. Juniper and palm trees loomed over small white statues representing the four seasons, and green hedges formed an uncomplicated maze, like in an English garden. A grey wagtail with its bright yellow belly hopped and then flew to the exposed, veiny roots of a massive banyan tree.

It is peaceful, here. Emma would have loved this space.

As Emma was dying, she and Robert had marked the time and the stages of the disease by the things she had lost—appetite, energy, and eventually her mind.

What if Emma, in her most difficult moment, had asked me to do what Chloe is asking?

The wagtail navigated the tree's roots, the bird moving without consideration for the deep ruts and crevices. How agile, Robert thought. No matter the unevenness, the bird's toes and small talons balanced its eager body with enviable nimbleness.

Emma would not have done such a thing. Her faith would never have permitted it. But could it have been the better thing to do? Might it had saved her from the indignity of struggling to swallow, from hearing her breath rattle, from watching her skin on her hands turn blue, from wetting the bed, from insisting she had seen the ghost of her long-dead mother standing at the bedroom doorway?

The wagtail hopped to the sidewalk again, its body motionless as its tail trembled. It snapped its head to one side and the other, assessing where it would go next, where its wings would take it. The bird lifted itself to the air and zig-zagged above the ground, fluttering up and over, down and back, acrobatic and lively. It landed on the grass near the hedges, pecking its beak at the ground, searching for insects, its tail, again, quivering to a blur.

Why does it do that? Why does its tail shudder? Maybe it's letting the predators know that there is no use in trying to catch me. I'm too quick for you. It's a waste of time. I will only make you appear a fool. Wouldn't it be wonderful if humans could do the same, signal to the predators—disease, tragedy, heartbreak— that we simply can't be caught? What a thing it would be if we were as quick as the wagtail.

Robert had promised himself he would see the bullring, and so he walked from the plaza to the Paseo de la Delicias toward the Paseo de Cristobal Colon, near the iron gates of the Catedral de Sevilla, eyeing the watercolors and silk scarves the vendors offered for sale from wooden booths. A bicyclist smiled as she passed on his left, unhurried, just as Robert had become. Time here would never be thought of as something to beat, to overcome. And it showed in his stride. It had taken Robert many days to find the unhurried pace. The change began in Granada, several days after arriving, as he walked to the plaza near his hotel in the late afternoon. He had forgotten his wristwatch, remembering it only when he had taken a seat at the cafe table near the church. Forgetting what had made him anxious. He had never been anywhere without his Timex, a gift from Emma on a birthday morning some thirty years ago. He considered going back to the hotel, but something stopped him. *It's safe on the tall dresser by the bed. No one is going to want my old watch.* And so, there and then, time became irrelevant. He ordered Sangria and didn't think of the watch again until he returned that night to again place the timepiece on his wrist. And now, as he stood before the entrance to the massive Plaza de toros de la Real Maestranza, its saffron-colored doors reminding him of blood, time again had become immaterial. It was not as if Robert didn't realize that he had decisions to make, and that there were limits to his contemplation, but here before this revered symbol of courage and art, this cathedral to what some have come to see as a barbaric blood sport and others steadfastly defending it as a morality play of high ceremony, time had no place. Instead, Robert considered only the bull and the matador, their mutual reverence, the metaphysical drama played out in a dance, marked not by the clock, but the timeless admiration of dual sacrifice, the matador's gamble with death and the bull's certainty of it. Robert recalled *Death in the Afternoon* and how Hemingway had praised this encounter, the heartbreak of it, how death would always come to find all of us. One should never apologize for bullfighting, the writer believed. For Hemingway and for Spain, bullfighting was not a sport. It was a tragedy. A great tragedy.

"Señor, there are no bullfights today."

Robert had been reading the large poster near the ticket window, detailing the dates of the fight and the matadors that would be featured when he noticed the man, gray of hair and walking with a cane, standing near him.

"There does not appear to be," Robert said.

"This is the break in the season," the old man said. "They return in September with the Feria de San Miguel."

"A big fair?"

"The grandest, señor."

The man was bent at the hip, the product of age, and he slumped forward as he stepped closer to the poster. He squinted through his glasses to read the names and dates.

"I came to three this year," the old man said.

"Are you from Seville?" Robert asked, turning to face the man. "Your English is good."

It was then that Robert noticed the taut and severely scarred skin below the man's left eye.

"I live here now. I am from Zaragoza. Where I was born," the old man said.

"But this is my home now. I live only block from these gates."

"You must love it," Robert said, motioning to the ring's main gate.

"It had been my life."

The old man looked again at the poster. "What does the bull see when he sees the matador?" he asked without answering. "He is only shadows, a target to rip apart. But this is the bull's instinct. Underneath the ferocity is a beating heart."

Robert knew then who was before him.

It had been a brutal goring. One of the most horrific in history, a horn to the face. Yet in only a few months, this matador was back in the bullring to face another great animal.

"I wore a black patch on my eye then," the old man said. "It became my signature."

"Where does courage like that come from?"

The old man smiled. "I was born for this. I know nothing else," he said. "I killed my first bull at the age of 12. I was a professional at 21. I knew only the ring and the bull."

"Your dignity is intact."

"My dignity is my heart and soul, he said, appearing to stand taller. "I have nearly died dozens of times. I have scars on my legs and arms, too. I see them every day and every night."

"And no regrets?"

"Never regrets, señor. There should never be regrets."

The old man pointed with his cane to the poster and a date in late September.

"I will return then, he said. Maybe you will?

"I've never seen a bullfight," Robert said.

"Ah, señor. You have not lived."

Robert shook the old man's hand, thanked him for his story, and stepped out from the Paseo de Colon. A small crowd had gathered at the entrance to a gift shop beyond the gates. At the doorway was a large, nearly life-sized plastic bull. A young boy stood before it, patting the bull's head and rubbing its horns. Maybe the boy was told this was good luck, Robert thought. Or maybe the boy was dreaming of something larger, something grand and brave. Maybe he was dreaming of what it might be like to face the charging bull, its lowered head, its flared nostrils, its wicked horns, and to hear the crowd cheering the graceful series of passes, and he, the matador, thrusting his sword between the bull's shoulder blades and watching it die.

15

It was nine o'clock. Early morning for Chloe after a night's work. She stood at the window to the street no longer able to sleep. Below was a dog, white and shorthaired, sniffing along the walkway. It must have had the scent of food, the drippings of meat from a pan emptied after a late dinner. Chloe's neighbor would often discard the remains of a meal into the street, the fat not good for the building's old pipes. And now, the dog, one Chloe had not seen before, had discovered unexpected pleasure.

Chloe had been reading a great deal. It was a way to distract her thoughts. She would read before sleeping, read before rising, read as she ate her bread and coffee. She had returned to books she had read in the past—as varied as Henry Miller's *Tropic of Capricorn* and Annie Dillard's *An American Childhood*. She found diversion in Stephen King's *Doctor Sleep* and was soothed by Mary Oliver's poems. She wasn't finishing most of what she started, reading several chapters, and stopping and moving to another book. She had returned to Shakespeare, too, although it was hard to fall into the rhythm of his words after so long. This morning, at the window, she held a worn paperback copy of Jim Harrison's *The Woman Lit by Fireflies*, containing three novellas, one, the *Sunset Limited*, a story of 1960s radicals reuniting to free an old friend from a Mexican jail. She had read it years ago, but this time considered putting it away as the book got too close to the bone. Still, she read, glancing between Harrison's words and the light in the window. The BBC played on the radio, low and nearly inaudible, although Chloe could make out portions of a news story about Northern Africa, some trouble in Algeria, a country that sounded so far away yet was just beyond the sea, Chloe reminding herself where she was, who she was, and who she had pretended to be. Like the radicals in the Harrison story, she too had attempted to create a different life for herself after dangerous days.

The dog had moved on from the window and a fat tabby cat had appeared. It sat hunched in the narrow street, tense, its ears folded back, and it began to show its teeth, silently snarling, its eyes focused on the edge of the white wall of the apartment building where the street twists to the left. The cat was motionless except for its mouth and whiskers. It snarled again and again. The dog must still be near, Chloe thought. She leaned closer to the window with her face to the pane, hoping to see along the street and detect what had disturbed the cat. At the corner, a movement of black. A shadow. A tail. Another cat emerged. Coal black. It had been out of view and now was slithering down the street. The tabby remained still, watching. Might one of the cats have been in heat? One trying to seduce, the other having none of it. Or maybe two tomcats fighting over a mouse, over territory. The fat tabby did not move until the black cat was out of sight. Then it turned and darted out of view along the street in the other direction. Chloe had seen street cats before but had not remembered this kind of encounter. It troubled her.

Chloe lit a candle and placed it on the sill. The candle had been purchased in a small store in Malaga some months ago. The candle held the scent of fir. Not a summer scent, Chloe thought, but one that soothed, nonetheless. As she began again to read, out of the corner of her eye, there came an old woman walking. At first, Chloe did not recognize the woman, but then did. The woman—hunched at the shoulders, her grey hair touched with darker natural highlights and dressed in an old flowing orange dress, a kind of old-fashioned house dress—carried two wicker baskets, the contents partially covered by red fabric. Chloe could see part of a loaf of bread in one, and in the other, maybe pears, apples, or mangos. The woman walked slowly along the street closest to Chloe's window. This was the woman who came often to Bar Lara carrying a basket much like the ones she had with her now but instead inside were necklaces and bracelets, handmade with sterling silver, leather, and colorful beads. The woman had long been an artisan and it was said that she had once owned a tiny shop in the Moroccan district, but she had aged, and now created her jewelry at home and sold it on the street. She offered it to those who sat at the tables, drinking sangria, smiling as she placed the pieces on a blue silk scarf before them. She was patient and kind. Chloe offered a wave of recognition. The old woman turned to the window, but the glare of the sun distorted her view, and she did not return the wave. The woman stopped and appeared to search the glass. Chloe waved again, and the woman's eyes widened. They were tired eyes, sapphire blue, and the contrast with her sun-darkened skin made them hard to ignore. The old woman placed one of her baskets on the ground before her, and with a bent and veiny hand she waved. The old woman bowed her head toward Chloe's image in the window and she blew a kiss, a gesture Chloe had not predicted. The woman smiled awkwardly, shyly. *How does she live her days?* Chloe thought. *Is she alone? Does she live well or in an old rundown apartment in the barrio? From where in her mind does she find her art? Does it come from pain? She had been to the market this morning, a long walk, an arduous walk for an old woman, down and then up the hill again. Was she sharing her goods, the bread, the fruit? Would this be her meal for the coming days?* The old woman bowed her head once again toward the window to offer a goodbye, and moved away with care, her hard black shoes meeting the ancient cobblestones until she had disappeared at the road's turn. *It's a simple life for her,* thought Chloe. *A happy one with simple days, knowing what each day would bring.* And it was then that guilt fell upon Chloe. It came with force and without warning. Guilt, an emotion she knew, one that had always be there, emerging in unforeseen ways. Shame, a form of guilt, is the most debilitating emotion, her mother once told her. When Chloe was in grade school, she had stolen another girl's lunch bag and hid it in the bushes near the school's entrance. A joke, she thought. The little girl trembled in tears, alone at her school desk, while others offered cookies, an apple, and half of a jelly sandwich from their own lunches. No one found out who had taken the lunch, and Chloe never confessed. Shame and guilt. What Chloe had done was not who she was, she wanted to believe, but she knew it was. We *are* what we do, even when we regret it, even when we know we have hurt, when the pain is unfixable.

16

Debbie had been a young girl when it happened. It was not until college that she learned all of it, what her father had done years ago in a time of weakness and uncertainty. The woman, some ten years younger than Robert, had worked with him at the grocery, one of the cashiers and an occasional assistant in the bakery. He had befriended her after learning of her son's death, a car accident, a horrible crash on a snowy night. They shared coffee and talked. He held her hand when she cried. The money he gave her had come from the family savings account, a hundred dollars at first, then two hundred, again and again, offered to her in cash to help with funeral expenses, to buy flowers and a small headstone. She was alone, this woman, the boy's father gone years before. When Emma had wondered aloud about the money, Robert had lied. Maybe it was for the tires the car needed, he had said. Maybe it was paying off the Christmas debt, he had said. You know me, he had said, I'm not so good with this kind of stuff. And each time he told another lie, he saw that woman's eyes, heard her voice, the way she thanked Robert for his help, his generosity.

He felt the hugs she had given him, the kiss on the cheek. He had offered money to a friend in need. It was nothing more than that, he insisted. But Robert knew it was more, knew it was different, and in time, Emma knew, too.

* * *

Debbie called her father in the afternoon.

"Are you giving her money, Dad?"

The question stung.

"I am not," Robert answered, a measure of timidity in his tone. "You asked this before, honey."

"You can be a softy."

"I'm really liking my trip and this country, and I wanted to be here a bit longer. That's all this is. I came to Seville and now I'm in Ronda." Robert stood on the balcony of his rented room near the ancient bridge that divides the city. "It's beautiful here."

"Where is she?"

"Granada."

"She didn't come with you?"

"No, she did not."

"Will you see her again?"

Robert knew the answer. But if he had said yes that would only bring more questions. "I'm not sure," he said.

"Did you have an argument with her?"

"Of course not."

"What do you mean, *of course not?*"

"She's been good to me."

"How?"

"Helpful. A good companion. I've told you so."

"And you're not giving her money?"

"Honey, please. I am not giving her money."

There was a pause and Debbie could hear her father inhale.

"She is asking me to do something for her," Robert continued.

As soon as he said this, he wanted to take it back.

"Dad?"

"Honey, this call must be costing you a lot of money."

"What is she asking you to do?"

"It's all right. I'm all right."

Now in Rhonda, in this medieval village, its white stone buildings clinging to the tall cliffs, with the late day sun still blazing, Robert thought both of the past and the future. Not what was present, what was untouchable, out of reach, as if nothing in the moment mattered. What mattered was the collective whole, all that he had become, all that had been determined by what he had been, how he allowed shame to remain in his blood, how it crippled him in ways he had never understood. And now, with whatever tomorrow would bring, whatever decision he would make, no matter what might appear as right and just, or even misguided or wrong, Robert's character would be evaluated. The present did not matter, for it would be here and gone in a flash, fast becoming yesterday and another stage on which to be judged.

After the phone call, Debbie wondered if she should get on a plane. An overreaction, she told herself. Still, she checked the flights to Madrid and the cost of a ticket. *What am I doing?* She asked herself. *Am I trying to save him? From what?* A foolhardy plan, she determined in time. She had seen her father's sadness after her mother died. Debbie recalled the first Christmas without her and how he had packaged a gift, wrapped it in red and green paper and tied a silver ribbon around the box. He handwrote a name tag—*To Emma*—and placed it under his small tree. When the season was over, the tree taken down and the ornaments put away, her father carried the small box in his car to the cemetery and left it at the gravesite. Debbie had never asked what was inside, and her father had never said. Now, with that remembrance and the sadness surrounding it, an uneasiness had returned. Her father's vulnerability had been exposed, a trait she had long adored but also one that had worried her.

* * *

Robert ordered oxtail and a bottle of red wine at the restaurant across the road from the bullring in Ronda. It was a restaurant of poets and writers, he was told. The head of a bull was mounted on the wall above the table, framed posters of great bullfights and legendary matadors had been closely arranged on the walls.

"Puedo servir el vino?"

The waiter was tall and thin. His hair gray and thinning. He wore a crisp white apron.

The wine, the color of deep cherries, delicately swirled in the glass and Robert took it to his nose. He had been embarrassed with this ritual when he first came to Spain. Wine had not been much a part of his life at home. Maybe some inexpensive chianti at Christmas or Easter but testing the wine's bouquet had never been part of the celebration. He wouldn't have known what he was supposed to experience, what he was expected to discover. Even now, when he had become more comfortable with the ceremony, Robert remained unsure of what was to be revealed. Still, he lifted the glass and closed his eyes.

"Bueno," Robert said.

"Si, señor."

As the waiter poured, he asked, now in English, if this was Robert's first time in Ronda, if he had been to the Puente Nuevo, the grand bridge above the steep chasm, and if he knew about the great bullring.

"Hemingway called it the most romantic town in Spain," the waiter said.

"Old Ernie loved this country, didn't he?" Robert asked, remembering why he had come to Spain in the first place.

"Are you here with a señorita?"

"All alone."

"One should not be alone in Ronda," the waiter said.

Robert thought of Emma. He thought of Debbie.

"Si. But I am." Robert lifted his glass and nodded.

"Disfrutar, señor."

"Gracias."

From his seat across from the large window, Robert could see the golden yellow of the tall plaza lamps outside the bullring entrance. The sky was darkening, and for a moment the busy street was empty, no one in sight, and his aloneness took over. He had hoped for clarity in the last days of travel but that was not what he was being offered. He had wanted clear insight, not what had come to him now, a kind of invisible yoke on his neck. *Why should I care? I should forget it all and book a flight home. I have no obligation to any of this.*

Robert poured another glass of wine. He dipped a piece of crusty bread into olive oil and tasted the earthiness.

"Your meal, señor."

The meal came on a large white plate, sprinkled with leeks and onions and garlic, in a brown broth, the meat slightly separating from the bone.

"Ah, beautiful. Bello."

"It is good luck, señor."

"Oxtail? Eating oxtail?"

"Si."

"Isn't everything good luck in Spain, mi amigo?"

"Do you need it, señor, this good luck?"

"Why not? I guess I do."

"Then it is so."

The aromas floated before him, and Robert began a silent prayer, something he hadn't done at meals since coming to Spain. He wondered why he hadn't and why a prayer had come to him now, the words as they had been so many times before, simple, and natural. Robert had said grace most nights before his dinners back home, as a man and a boy, and now here he was, weeks into this trip whispering petitions for the first time. He was ashamed, saying grace again, only now when he had found himself lowdown, in need of greater guidance. But as the street through the window began to slowly fill again with people, and laughter and song returned to the ancient town; when the Spanish night had fully come and had reawakened and the lamps in the plaza grew brighter; when the spotlight outside Spain's ancient bullring had beamed on the statue of Antonio Ordonez, the matador who had faced more than 3000 bulls and lived, within Robert emerged a radiance of thought, an unforeseen newness. What he had been careful to conceal, albeit unknowingly, was now directly before him, pure and fully formed.

17

As Chloe readied for the night shift at Bar Lara, she felt it coming on. First her fingers tingled, then her forearms. The tremors never manifested in the same way, but she knew. Sometimes she felt them in the legs first. She had noticed spasms in the back of her eyes once, or so it seemed that way. And so, with this, she took her pills. She swallowed and closed her eyes and hoped. At the bar, the tremors subsided enough for her to work, enough to serve wine and tapas and to somehow smile.

The weather had been cooler than usual and maybe that's why it was a slow night. To pass the time, she brought along reading. When she was younger, she was insatiable, devouring books, sometimes one a week. That had been abandoned long ago. Still, she had found reading had separated her from her thoughts. When patrons were not beckoning, she read, a handful of words at a time, enough to transport her for a little while. This night it was Shakespeare. Chloe had wanted to switch gears after reading a novel and the Irish writer, Roddy Doyle, a story of two old friends drinking their way around Dublin, a moving book, but nothing like Shakespeare. Chloe knew what she was in for when she began *Othello*. She knew the story. Had seen the play years ago. She knew it was not going to end well.

"Excuse me. señorita," the man said. He sat alone at a table in the plaza close to bar's entrance, smoking, drinking red. "Do you always read here?"

Chloe stood from her chair near the kitchen's window and hurried to the man's table.

"I'm sorry, señor. What can I get you?"

The man's accent was English, refined but unpretentious. Big man. Not fat, just big. White beard. Wore a large-brimmed straw hat, his unruly hair tumbled from the sides to the tops of his ears. He sunk heavy in his seat, a wrinkled seersucker jacket hung loosely from his shoulders, and covered a white linen shirt slightly frayed at the collar.

"Oh, no, señorita. No need. I was simply wondering. The reading?"

Chloe had placed the book on the seat of her chair before attending to the man. She looked back at it.

"Yes, I read here sometimes. I try not to let it distract me here. Sorry again."

"And your boss?"

"He doesn't mind. And he's not here tonight."

"And the story you read?"

"Shakespeare," Chloe said, her voice softening, as if not wanting to reveal her choice.

"Ah, which one? *A Midsummer Night's Dream*, I might bet."

"*Othello*."

"Goodness, my dear."

"Not exactly light."

"Adultery. Betrayal. Death."

"I'm at the end of Act One."

"But surely you know."

Chloe wiped her fingers across her lips. "I know the play, yes," she said.

"A lovely woman in a beautiful country on a stunning Spanish night reading such tragedy."

The man swallowed the last from his glass and returned it to the tabletop. Chloe reached for the wine bottle.

"May I?" she asked, tilting the bottle's neck toward the rim. There was the unmistakable delicate sound of liquid on glass amplified in the evening.

"What is your name, my dear?" the man asked.

The answer came without hesitation, as if Chloe was again a little girl, summoned by the teacher to answer the call of attendance. The answer like a reflex, as the crystal vase begins to tumble from one's hands, sliding out from the fingers in slow motion without regard for time. The hands clench and reach, but it is impossible to keep the glass from crashing to the ground, shattering into shards.

"Megan, she said. My name. It's Megan."

* * *

Chloe would not sleep well that night. Most nights, an hour after returning home she had closed her eyes and was soon dreaming. But not this night. She was unsettled, probing and questioning. She read and read some more—finishing *Othello*, then several acts in *Julius Cesar* and *Anthony and Cleopatra* and *Romeo and Juliet*. And then she searched for literary interpretations on the internet, the words of scholars on Shakespeare's tragedies, his themes, researching and comparing, moving back and forth between Shakespeare's words and professorial explorations. In time, hunched over the light of a single lamp, Chloe saw it clearly. It was plain. So obvious. Why wouldn't Shakespeare have considered another way? Why wouldn't this great mind have offered something better than poisons, daggers, and hopelessness? Chloe turned her head to the window facing the street. Shadows danced along the shades. *Maybe,* she thought, *maybe he knew the futility of it all, and maybe he knew exactly what he was doing.* Chloe leaned back in her chair, lifted her chin, and sighed. She didn't want to cry but crying came anyway. And in her upper thigh, a quiver, and another closer to her calf. She placed the medicine on her tongue and swallowed. Tension in her neck; a clenched jaw. Chloe placed her head in her hands, inhaled, and wiped perspiration from her upper lip. Another pill on the tongue. And then another. In her palm she held a fourth and a fifth and a sixth and a seventh. The warm sweat on her palm had dissolved a bit of the capsules' red dye, staining her hand. And then, sudden words in the middle of the night. A text. It was 3:45 a.m.

coming back. can we talk tomorrow?

Chloe allowed the pills fall from her hand to her lap, one at a time, ran her fingers through her hair from forehead to crown, closed her eyes, and shook her head. "Robert," she whispered, "you don't really get the texting thing, do you?"

She stood over the sink and drank two glasses of tap water and put herself to bed.

18

At the top of the hill near the market, Robert sat in a heavy iron chair, black, the same color as the small table next to it. It was at the north end of the plaza, close to the street but not where it can sometimes be busy, especially in the morning. The market merchants moved slowly, setting up their wooden tables, hauling crates from the beds of small trucks. Robert watched a man and young girl, maybe a father and daughter, working meticulously, stacking Pomegranates in pyramid style, and placing bread, dusted white with flour at intricate angles so that the crusty ends reached out of the baskets.

Robert had returned to Granada two days before. Chloe wanted a public place to talk, somewhere in the open. Robert had suggested otherwise, something private, but meeting at his hotel or her apartment was too intimate for Chloe, too close. Choosing Robert came from her innate trust in him, but also because he could remain distant, she thought, and she could stay detached. That was the purpose, to keep the heart out of it. But as Robert sat alone waiting, he considered their unexpected bond, Chloe's graciousness, her generosity, and how the unanticipated promise between them came from beyond their powers—unseen, untouchable, uncalculated.

It was then that he saw her, walking from the far end of the plaza. She wore a simple blue dress that showed her shoulders. The dress caught the breeze and lifted slightly above her knees. He had never seen Chloe dressed this way before. Robert felt the pulse of something, as one does when rising to the crest of hill back home, in the mountains and forests and viewing for the first time the expanse of the winding river below, the pines carpeting the hills, a wide-angle lens of surprise.

Chloe surveyed the tables and found him. She waved from the hip.

"Hola," she said as she arrived tableside.

Robert, standing, maneuvered a second chair to the small table. "It's good to see you," he said.

"It's good to see you, too."

Chloe's eyes met Robert's then turned away, looking past him to the woman selling flowers along the cobblestone walkway. Robert pretended to watch a vendor selling a brown bag of peaches to an old man.

"Do you want a tea, coffee?" Robert asked, gesturing toward the cafe.

Thinking for a moment, Chloe shook her head. There was a beat of silence

and then another.

"So," Robert said

"Would you mind if I talk first?" Chloe asked. She folded her hands, placed them on the table, and sighed. "My dad was a carpenter," she began.

For nearly an hour, Chloe unveiled her life, pulling back curtains on an autobiography she had been waiting to tell but never could. Not because it was too painful; not because she had never wanted to open up; not because she had never wished to share. She simply did not believe it was a story worth telling. The only one who has any stake in the telling is the one telling it, she had believed. *All of us have our own stuff. Why would anyone want to suffer through mine when they have their own?* Still, she knew that in time, somewhere and some way, she would be ready to let it out.

Her mother and father went to high school together. They married at a small steepled church in Augusta, Georgia. In less than year, Megan was born. She was named after her parental grandmother. On her birthday, the young Megan had wispy blonde hair, like her mothers, but in time it darkened, the color of the bark of an oak tree.

"We never had money," she continued. "Dad built houses. Then the market wasn't so good, and he began building outdoor decks on expensive homes in Summerville.

Chloe played as most kids did growing up, riding bikes, and climbing on backyard swing sets where her friends lived. She was in a softball league, but she never was good at the game. By high school, she quit, and in her sophomore year, her father left.

"One morning he wasn't there. My mother told me he was on a job in Birmingham. Then it was a job in Atlanta. And one in Pensacola. On and on."

An absent father didn't make Chloe so different; other girls she knew had similar stories. In time, she became angry and that made things different. Not all the girls were as angry, instead simply giving up on whatever the heart had held onto. In time, Chloe learned her mother had been lying to her. And in the realization, she considered taking a bus to Florida to search for her father but didn't have enough money to last more than a few days and gave up the idea. She also wasn't certain where he was if he was there at all. A year later at Christmas, a card arrived, a cheap old-fashioned holiday card with red cardinals on the front. It was addressed to "the family" and inside was a note, only a few words. Her father was in Texas "visiting his brother" and missed everybody "so much." Chloe didn't believe a word of it, and she tried to forget. In the weeks after the holiday, her mother lost weight, joined a yoga class at the community center, began making jewelry—bracelets out of ceramic beads—and reading books on Buddhism she had borrowed from the library.

"She got pregnant sometime that summer," Chloe said. "It was a girl. So, I have a sister. Nineteen years younger than me."

Chloe took a few classes at the community college and then the University of Kansas. She became a middle school teacher for a time in Lawrence, helped run a gift shop in Denver, volunteered with a missionary group in Guatemala, taught Pilates in Austin, tended bar in Eugene. It was in Oregon that she joined a small environmental group helping to plant trees in the eastern part of the state.

"I got really into it," she said. "It meant something. Some of the best days of my life. Some of the best people I've ever met."

A week before the protest and fire, there was a phone call from her mother. Her father was dead, his body found in a

Mexican border town. He had collapsed in the dirt outside a bar in Los Algodones.

"I still remember the name of the place. Las Parrilla," she said. After that, I found out about the disease. He apparently had had it for years."

It was the last time she spoke with her mother.

"It all become something different, and after those days in Oregon, well, I had to become someone else. And you know the rest of that story."

Robert reached to touch her hand.

"I'm okay," she said. "I just needed to get all of this out, all of it straight, you know, in my head. And, I have to be sure."

"You can be sure. You can. But there's still the how and the when? How is this all going to go forward?"

"I have the medicine. I've told you that," she said, thinking for a moment. "Seems an odd word to use—*medicine*."

"When do you think?"

"Soon."

"And you're okay? I mean, you seem okay."

"I don't want to wait. I don't want to get to where I have no control. And what would I be waiting for?"

"I can't be there. You know this."

"I will have all the paperwork, the documents, the people to contact. Phone numbers that I know of. Addresses, at least the last ones I know about. And, yes, I will go away on my own. I know where. I have it worked out. North of here. Two days will pass, and it will be over. You won't hear from me. And then, you can move on."

Robert had considered this moment, this conversation, preparing for the weight of it. The uncertainties. But instead of being shaken, he found himself oddly relieved. He had made his own decision about it, come to an agreement with himself. Or maybe he had only convinced himself of this. And now, it seemed Chloe, too, he had come to her own terms about it all, was resigned to what was before her, and despite it all, the world was still spinning around.

"It's all rather unremarkable, isn't it?" Chloe said, standing and adjusting the dress strap over her left shoulder. "A life. This life. We all have them. And we're all the same, you know? Desperately alone."

"Un momento," Robert said, raising his right hand and his index finger. He stood from the small table, chose a single gazania with its vibrant petals of orange and yellow from the woman selling flowers at the corner, and handed it to Chloe. "For all the lonely people," he said.

Chloe brought the flower close, put it to her nose, and tucked it behind her ear.

"You look beautiful," Robert said. He ached to embrace her, to hold her head on his shoulder, to allow her to cry, to shudder in his arms, to open the ache inside.

"It's so strange," Chloe said, "having control over your own destiny, or the end of it. Truth is, I'm still trying to figure that out. Not sure you really can. But it's not about how or when or if I must do this. I already know the answers to those questions."

"I want you to be, what do people say—at peace with it?"

"Can anyone really be?"

In the silence that came next, Robert heard in his head the words Chloe had said moments before: *Rather unremarkable.* He thought of his mother and how she had always reminded him when he was a boy of how special he was, that he could do no wrong. How he would do great things someday. Robert had said the same to his daughter, Debbie, and all good parents in the world had done the same, reminded their children of their worth. He did not doubt the words or their intentions, the good they were meant to do. But when time is running out, we all realize in some way that our lives are unexceptional. There is joy and reward and beauty in a life, we make our mark somehow, but in our search for the extraordinary, we discover instead vulnerability and how wonderfully ordinary all of us are.

"I must be crazy," Chloe said, wiping moisture from the corner of her eye. "It's so terribly unfair what I am asking from you."

"You need not worry."

Chloe touched her tiny stud earrings one at a time, as if to be sure they were still there. She turned away and back again to Robert, her eyes narrowing, as if trying to hold back everything inside.

"It's okay," Robert said.

"It'll be after the weekend. Monday."

"All right."

"I'll have everything for you by tomorrow. Everything you need."

Robert nodded.

"Funny," Chloe said, giving herself a moment to think. "It's a bit strange to say that word. *Tomorrow.*" She smiled. "Now, aren't I being melodramatic?"

Chloe walked across the plaza, through the tables and the center of the market now busy with shoppers and disappeared along the cobblestone walkway. And Robert took the long way back to the hotel, down the steep side of the hill, tight against the buildings on the narrow street—the straw hat he had purchased when he had arrived weeks ago pulled down to shadow his eyes—remaining in the shade as he walked, the glorious shade, like any good Spaniard would do on a hot summer day in Granada.

19

The sun on the face may keep out the shadows, but the wind, it gives much more. It reminds us that we are alive. And it was the wind, this reminder of life, that was first to greet Robert on Sunday morning when he stepped from his hotel and walked through the plaza near the old church, down the steep streets of cobblestone, and beyond the balconies above where pots of red geraniums sat against the black iron railings. It was a light wind, but enough to be the quiet morning's singular sound. The breeze met him at the street corner. There was a delicate rush between the old apartment buildings, and a moderate gust as he stepped into the plaza in front of the cathedral. It was impossible to tell from which direction the wind was coming, he only knew he could not avoid it. The wind would not leave him alone.

The cathedral bells rang. Echoes of morning. And echoes of the church back home, thousands of miles away. The clang cut through the morning as parishioners waited on the steps outside. An old man stood alone near the massive doors, his eyes closed, rubbing black prayer beads. He kissed the silver cross at the end of the chain, gathered the beads in his hand, and as the door opened, he slowly moved inside, the first to enter. Robert stood in the plaza, watching, and when the last of the crowd was gone, he looked to the sky, and ascended the steps. He took the last pew on the left, sitting near the end of the row. He knelt, closed his eyes, and made the sign of the cross. A choir sang in Latin—sweet, high tones. Like young angels, Robert thought. More parishioners moved down the center aisle, finding seats. From behind and to his left on the outside aisle, Robert sensed a presence.

"You have returned," a voice said. It was the young nun he had spoken with shortly after arriving in Granada. "May I?" she asked.

Robert, recognizing her now, allowed room for her to sit at the pew's end.

"You remember me," he said.

"Si, señor. It was not hard."

The comment puzzled Robert, but it would have been awkward to ask for an explanation.

The nun smiled and looked about the cathedral. "It is so beautiful, no?"

Very much," Robert said.

"So many come because of its beauty, and I pray that this beauty helps them to think inside," she said, placing her hand on her heart.

Robert lifted his eyes to the gold ceiling.

"You, señor? You are here for the *inside* this time?"

"I guess I am. I mean, yes, I am."

"Special intentions?"

Robert nodded.

"So many come feeling they must. Do you know this?"

"I suppose so."

"The guilt of forgetting God, the guilt of not forgiving, the guilt of not living a life God might want us to live."

Robert remembered his night in Ronda, his dinner alone across from the bull ring. "Shame and guilt," he said.

"It is a powerful emotion, no?"

"It is."

"And you, señor, do you carry the cross?"

Robert leaned forward, placing his chin to his chest, and closing his eyes. "Oh, sister, I think I do," he said.

"You are not alone, señor. Know this."

"But I feel I am."

The nun remained silent for several moments.

"Your heart, señor, is your compass. I can see this in you."

"But it's not only me. Not all about me," he said, hesitating for a moment. "It's my friend, too."

"I pray for your friend, señor. I pray for you."

Robert offered a shy smile.

"We run from it, this death. We are like all God's creatures," the nun continued. "Fight, flight, or freeze, no? Our existence is threatened, and we act, we panic, we are sad and terrified. This is what we do."

The choir was quiet, and the murmurs of the parishioners had faded.

"El Señor este contigo," the priest announced, his hands raised to the congregation, his solemn old face emotionless.

The voices in the cathedral returned his words.

"Levantan sus corazones," the priest continued.

"Los levantamos al Señor," the voices replied.

"But sister," Robert whispered, leaning close. "I believe God has failed me."

"Death is not the cure for our shame, our guilt," the sister said. "Life is where suffering may always be, but death cannot solve this. There is eternity, señor."

"I'm not sure I believe in the afterlife anymore," Robert whispered.

The nun knelt, crossed herself, closed her eyes. "Pray, señor."

The cathedral appeared darker than the first time he had visited, dim in the corners, and the faces of those inside full of sorrow. The priest said in Spanish, "Lord God, Lamb of God, Son of the father. You take away the sins of the world." After all the masses, the thousands and thousands of psalms, readings, gospels, and homilies since Robert's childhood, through his days as a young man, his marriage, the birth, and baptism of his daughter, he had been unable to find the comfort he thought would come. He held the cathedral's leather-bound hymnal in his hand, the one he had hoped to sing from, pronouncing the words as best he could. But now all he could do was massage its frayed edges.

"Forgive me, sister," Robert said, "I must go."

Robert walked through the plaza toward the Parque Federico Garcia Lorca and then through the streets at the center of town. He found an English language bookstore on Calle Primavera, one of the few places open, and purchased *The Oxford Shakespeare: The Complete Works*. That night, Robert read *Hamlet* and cried.

***

The phone rang before the sun was up.

"Dad? Can you hear me?"

"Debbie, honey. Is everything all right?"

Robert sat up in bed and turned on the low light of the lamp on the nightstand where his phone had been.

"I know it's early. What, 6 a.m. or so?"

"Yes, I think so. What's going on, honey?" Robert asked, sleep in his voice.

"I'm okay, Dad. But are *you* okay? I had a horrible feeling all night."

"No. No. I'm good. I'm fine."

"I was so anxious."

"Oh, honey."

"I'm sorry."

When Emma was in her final weeks, telephone calls had been demons. Making them, receiving them had been dreadful. Robert was either telling someone bad news or getting it. Phones ringing at odd hours had made his bones shake, his heart twinge. Phone calls from doctors and hospitals, Robert making phone calls to tell friends and family to tell them how Emma had been that day. Death was coming and Robert was certain its arrival would be announced through a phone call; one that would be made in the middle of the night, in the hours when sleep had once given him peace. Emma died in the early hours of a Tuesday morning, long before dawn. Earlier that day Debbie had been with Robert at Emma's bedside, a vigil, knowing the time would soon come in hours or maybe, a doctor had said, in days. Robert had insisted Debbie go back home that night to her own bed, rest as best she could. There would be time to say goodbye, he told her. When Emma died Robert had to phone his daughter with the news in the wee hours of a dark morning. Now, hearing Debbie's anxiety, Robert tried to find the lightness in his voice, a tone of brightness, a sign to show that all was well. He spoke of his trip to Seville and the beautiful gardens he saw, the bullring, the good food, the smiling faces. He told of Ronda's ancient bridge and the good wine and Hemingway. The hundreds and hundreds of olive trees and the unrelenting warm sun, its brilliance, and how Spaniards always searched for shade.

"I'm so glad you've learned to love the country," Debbie said. "But when are you coming home?"

"Soon, honey."

"This has to be expensive and the change of flights, and more hotel nights."

"I have one more thing here to do."

"What?"

For days Robert had told white lies. Now he had opened a door to the truth, and he was lost.

"I hope you feel better. I'm good, honey. I really am. Still nice to hear your voice."

"Hearing you now is good, too, Dad. But what's this one thing you're going to do?"

Robert wanted to hang up. He wanted to hide. Instead, he reached for a question he knew he believed he might regret, a question of hopeless distraction, a question that had been there, waiting, a long time to be asked.

"This may seem, well, out of place after all the time going by and all, but it's been on my mind."

Robert's mouth was dry.

"When your mother died, I never saw you cry," he said.

"Dad? Of course, I cried. Why are you asking this?"

"Maybe alone you did, I guess. But you saw me cry. I never saw you."

"What is this about?"

"I've been thinking about your mother here. I guess she's on my mind."

"But that question. Really?""

"Please, don't be mad."

"I was an absolute mess. I still cry."

Robert knew Debbie had wept on her own, but tears never came when anyone was looking.

"Death is so odd," he said.

"What does that mean?"

"Forget it, honey. All of it. Forget what I said."

"Dad, are you okay?"

"I am. Sure. Yes. I am."

After a moment of silence, she said, "I guess we all find our own ways to fall apart."

Robert wanted to go back in time. But it was done. And there they were, the two of them, all alone, and far apart.

"She lives on in you," Robert said.

"I know, Dad, I'm her immortality, aren't I?"

Robert promised to call in a day or two with his plans for coming back, when she could meet him at the airport. And before hanging up, he told Debbie how much he loved her—something he needed to say more than she needed to hear. Robert turned off the lamp and as he placed his head to the pillow once again, he could not forget the night he sent Debbie home too early.

20

Chloe had arranged her things as if she were preparing for a weekend away. On the bed was a small canvas satchel. It held two old cotton t-shirts, both black, ones she sometimes slept in, two pairs of shorts, one tan and the other white. Two pairs of panties, one white the other black. She had taken everything out of her purple makeup bag and replaced what had been there with a tin of lip balm and a toothbrush. *What's the point?* she thought, smiling, and holding the brush her in hand for a moment. She placed it inside anyway. And in the side pocket of the satchel, wrapped in hand cloth, she had packed the small stone Indalo carving, the one from the rented apartment near Velez Blanco where she and Robert had traveled. Chloe had taken it from the shelf above the bed before leaving. *I will return it, someday,* she had thought then. She knew now that would never happen. Also, in the satchel, the blue dress she had worn on the morning she met Robert at the market. It would the last thing she would wear along with a necklace, a gift from her mother many years ago, a small white pearl on a silver chain. She wore it as she zipped the satchel closed. After lighting a candle and placing it on her nightstand, Chloe rested on the bed, her packed bag at her side, her eyes open to the ceiling.

* * *

It was a short walk back to the hotel, and Robert had swayed from one side of the narrow cobblestone street to the other, stumbling once, nearly falling. He fumbled for the key to his room, dropping it twice to the tile floor, the hard clang echoing in the courtyard. He had finished a bottle of cheap tempranillo at Mirador, Marques de Riscal, sitting at a table with a view of all of Granada below. After it was empty, he ordered another bottle, an expensive cabernet—Mas la Plana. He knew he was overdoing it. Halfway through, his stomach turned. He ate bread, drank water, and rested. In time, Robert poured another glass. He drank it slowly, paid his bill, and carried with him the bottle of what little remained, only to watch it slip from his hands to the cobblestone as he exited the restaurant door, glass shattering at his feet. In the dim light, he kicked away what he could see of the shards from the walkway toward the wall of the stone building, and with sweat along his temples, embarrassed and nauseous, he walked to the hotel, attempting to stay in a straight line and dodging headlights form one car and another. And now alone in his room, he, like Chloe, was in bed, eyes open to the ceiling. *This is how I will die*, he thought. *Disoriented, starring into nothing.* Robert thought of Emma and her last days. He thought of all the time that had passed, living in his small world, a tiny dot on Earth.

And he saw himself looking down from heaven to a world he failed to fully see or understand, and he thought he might cry.

* * *

A number of papers and documents had been placed in a manila envelope. There was the key to her apartment and a note asking that all that remained be donated to the thrift shop at the cathedral. There was the apartment lease and euros tucked inside a small white envelope, money to pay the last of the rent. Along with a photograph of Chloe—several years old, smiling as she stood before the cave carvings—she had written on yellow-lined paper the last address of her sister, and the name of a man who had been part of the group of environmentalists in Oregon. Below this was the address of the U.S. Embassy in Madrid. There was also a recent newspaper clipping of the debate in the Spanish parliament over euthanasia—the fight to legalize it, the efforts by Catholics to stop it. And on neatly folded white paper, details of what to do with her body—cremation, the remains to be scattered near the caves in Velez Blanco, if possible— and along with the note, wrapped with a rubber band, 800 Euros to cover what costs there may be. Chloe was not asking Robert to fulfill these wishes himself, only that someone, anyone, would or could. She sealed the envelope and placed it on top of the satchel, Robert's name written in pen on the outside. From her position on the bed, Chloe rested her left hand on the envelope, as if to secure it, and keep it safe. After a time, she closed her eyes. She was tired, weary, together with it an odd sort of comfort. She blew out the candle and fell asleep on top of the bedspread with her clothes still on.

*   *   *

Robert could hear music. It came from outside. Muffled and faint. A guitar and a voice, low and scratchy. *It's the old man*, he thought, the man who hunches over his guitar and leans his frail body against the wall along the walkway to the market. Robert had seen him before, noting his long gray beard and his matted hair, his dirty denim pants. There was nothing special about his playing, only that he was always there on Robert's walk to the plaza and the market, always moving from one corner to another offering songs. And now, in the low light and through the hotel walls, Robert had recognized the sound, the music of the old man, singing in Spanish. *He must have been playing tonight in the plaza*, Robert thought, *asking for money, his battered guitar case opened for coins.* And now, the old man was walking home, singing, and playing along the ancient streets in the dark, as Robert drifted into the hours after midnight.

21

It was the heat of the day, and few sat in the plaza. An older woman read a book under the shade of a canopy. A husband and wife from Germany, Robert guessed from the accent, drank sangria. And on his other side, two tables away, a young woman, a local, he presumed, smoked cigarettes, and drank white wine. Robert sat closest to the steps of the old church, under a large umbrella, across the table from an empty chair.

Chloe had not yet arrived.

It was where they had met, in this plaza, at Bar Lara. Maybe that's why she chose it, or maybe it was simply familiar. She was at home here in this plaza high above Granada. Chloe wanted a public place, somewhere out in the open, and this was that place. Fewer chances to get emotional, she had said.

Robert ordered bottled water and an espresso. It had been a fitful night, and he slept late, missing breakfast at the hotel. His head ached, and although an obligatory toast or final words might require alcohol, a drink was the last thing he wanted. What he wanted was a sign, something that assured him, something clear and complete. So much was unreal and upside-down. He thought about his father, the words he would say when Robert showed apprehension, when he was unsure. *You got this.* Robert could hear him now, clear, and direct. *You got this.* He had said it when Robert took his first high school job cutting grass at a golf course, he said it in the hours before he was to ask Emma to marry him, he said it as Robert watched his baby girl through the glass in a hospital ward hours after her birth.

You got this.

This was nothing his father could imagine.

Chloe arrived from Robert's right. He could see her silhouette now as she made her way across the plaza from the stone walkway and steps near the overlook to the city.

"I've been out most of the morning," Chloe said as she stood before the empty chair at Robert's table. "Early on, before sunrise. Those first few moments of the day. They are so special and so brief."

Robert stood as Chloe took her seat.

"Granada is glorious, haven't I come to know. Especially on a summer morning," Robert said.

Chloe placed the manila envelope she had prepared on the table.

"Do you want to talk about this right away?" she asked.

Robert thought for a moment. "I assume it's all pretty clear," he said.

"I hope so."

"I'll see it when I need it. You okay with that?"

"There are some things to tidy up. Not much, really. Some money for what is needed. But. Robert, please, I know this is hard. If you find you can't do this, can't go through with it, give it to those who find me."

"But won't they know then that I knew?"

"Leave it in my apartment, then. The key is inside. But you might want to put it in a different envelope," Chloe said, pointing to Robert's name written on outside.

Robert nodded.

"You can still say no," she said.

"And what would that do at this point?"

"Nothing. I guess."

"I've made the decision."

"And I have, too."

A room had been secured in Zujaira, 20km north of Granada. Two nights at the Casa Grande, a room dressed in white linen, white floor tile, and a window to the gardens. She would think, journal, maybe pray, she told Robert. There was a small library there, books to read, and a lovely stone pool where she could swim long after the sun fell. Night swimming. It would be quiet and beautiful.

"In two days, I will be gone," Chloe said. "On the third day, you can call and ask for a wellness check."

Robert rubbed his eyes. "And you know what you're doing with this drug?" Robert asked.

Chloe reached to touch his hand. "I do," she said.

"And what if it doesn't work?"

"It will, Robert. It will."

Robert watched as two old women climbed the stone steps to the church. "That's where I'm going when you walk away," he said. "I don't think God likes me much right now."

"God understands," Chloe said. Her hand remained on Robert's, and she held it tighter. "I had a dream last night," she said.

Chloe was falling, falling. No sky, no ground. Nothing to grasp. But she wasn't rushing through the air, she was floating, like the seeds of a dandelion. The wind first carrying her and then letting her drop, carry and drop, over and over. Her body light and fragile. Her arms like feathers. A single red flower in her hair that the wind could not remove. And in her hand, as she fell, she massaged three small stones, rubbed smooth and shiny, clicking as they touched, a strange and beautiful music.

"I was at peace, Robert."

Robert covered his mouth with his hand.

"I'm in a good place," Chloe added.

Robert closed his eyes and inhaled. "Forgive me. But I have to ask," he said, his face flushing. "Is there more to this?"

Chloe tilted her head.

"Your disease. Is it only an excuse?" Robert continued.

Chloe squinted.

"You have time, Chloe. You have time before it gets bad. Before you can't function. You can still enjoy this life. What is left. That incredible Granada morning, those first moments, there are many still left for you."

"You think there's another reason I want to die?"

"That sounds harsh."

"It's what you're asking. Do you think this is some pathetic will of mine? Do you think this comes out of pity?"

"No. No."

"You don't think I have looked at everything? You don't think I'm torn up inside? You don't think I'm broken? I'm broken, Robert. Broken all over."

"I'm so sorry," Robert said. "I shouldn't have."

"I have asked extraordinary things of you. Just say no, then. I will understand."

"This is the last thing I wanted on this day."

"And you think I did?"

"Forgive me," Robert whispered.

The church bells rang out and Robert looked to the tower.

Chloe reached inside the pocket of her shorts and placed a small package on the table. She motioned for Robert to unwrap it. He unfolded the white crepe paper and found the small stone Indalo, the one she had stolen. For a moment, Robert could not breath. Chloe's smile came slowly. She kissed Robert's hand, stood, turned, and walked the short distance beyond the church, disappearing in the shadows that the sun had formed.

* * *

That night, Robert returned to the plaza to hear the street music and drink pacharán before bed, a liqueur he had been offered in Rhonda and found he liked. On the far side near the overlook, a young man in dreadlocks and baggy pants played the fiddle, his body swaying in dreamy rhythms. Robert hoped the drink, the night air, and the music might settle his head and help him eventually find sleep. The night air was heavy from a hot day, and combined with the warmth of his drink,

Robert sank into his chair, his body giving in, his mind floating in and out of memories—the day he and Emma moved into their home on Piedmont, a Sunday afternoon Pirate game when Debbie was just a young girl, fireworks on the last night of the arts festival at Point Park when he, Emma, and Debbie rested in the grass and looked to the sky in awe. And a day at the beach as a boy when he tested his mother's instincts and his will.

Robert was in the shallow waters of Lake Erie. It was a late summer family trip to Presque Isle after several Saturday swimming lessons at the municipal pool near home. His mother waded close by, the light of a hot August sun glinting on the tips of the waves. Robert was to test what he had learned, to release his body forward and stroke his arms, level his head to the waterline, and take deep breaths in and then hold them, and release them again. The lake was calm, but its vastness was unmistakable. In the distance there was nothing but water, the color of slate melting into the horizon. *Do what you have done before*, his mother said. *Do what you have been taught.* He felt the resistance of the waves against his thighs as he stepped deeper into the lake, and when the water reached his chest, he lifted his feet from the sand below, inhaled, closed his eyes, and allowed himself to sink below the surface. The caw of seagulls fell silent, the pressure was like plugs in his ears. For a moment, Robert thought he was drowning, unsure of where he was. But he leveled his body and his legs kicked and his arms cut through the water, his body rose, and as he turned his head to catch air, he heard his mother call. *Not too far. Stay where I can see you, where you can touch bottom.* But Robert was strong now, and he swam farther from the shore, one stroke after another, his arms like flippers, his feet like rudders. He tasted the musky water and felt the sun's heat on his neck. *How far to the other side? How far to Canada?* And when his body could stroke no more and he became breathless, he lowered his feet and found nothing. No solid ground. So, he kicked, and beat the water with his skinny arms, holding his body afloat, just as he had learned at the pool. Along the shore he could see his mother, standing knee deep frantically waving for him to return, her voice muffled. Robert watched her for a moment and began to laugh, lifted an arm to return the wave, the kind of wave adventurers give from the deck of an ocean-bound ship pulling away from shore. And as Robert now considered the memory, he wondered where that boy had gone.

The fiddler had finished his song. He bowed and walked with his open fiddle case to the few remaining patrons at the plaza tables. "Gracias," he said as coins were tossed inside. "Es muy amable de tu parte." He stood before Robert. "Señor? Que seas tan amble?"

Robert lifted his eyes to the musician. "Young man," he said, "you play beautifully. Don't ever stop playing." Robert pulled from his front pocket neatly folded euros and tossed several notes into the fiddler's case.

"Ah. Señor. Your generosity. Gracias."

"Do you promise?" Robert asked.

"Si. Si. Lo prometo."

Robert believed, for now, he could sleep.

22

From the tall open window of her room, where long white curtains hung to the floor, Chloe could see the mountains. The misty light of the falling sun had turned the hills into giant shadows across the horizon. Outside and below her second-floor space, she heard voices in Spanish—a man and a woman, whispering and then giggling, lovers who had been to the house's other side to watch the sunset and had come now to the east side to steal away in the coming dark. The voices were sweet and happy, and they had allowed Chloe to forget for a moment.

She had considered writing a long goodbye note, words for someone, anyone, but dismissed the thought. Instead, she had spent the evening meticulously arranging the room, placing a vase of flowers the staff had delivered, a welcome touch for all guests, on the small table where she could see them from the bed, and turning down the white bedspread, the top right corner pulled to the shape of a perfect triangle. She had placed two pillows, one on top of the other at the headboard. Her clothes had been packed away in the satchel, all but the blue dress she wore and the pearl necklace around her neck. Chloe was barefoot, and to match the dress and her nails of her fingers, she had painted her toenails blue, one of last things she did before leaving Granada. She thought of that now, standing at the window. *What an odd thing to have done, to consider, the color of one's toenails.* And near the lamp on the nightstand, she had placed a glass of water and the pillbox. And now, at the window, a fresh breeze fluttered the curtains and touched her face, and for the first time in a long time she had forgiven herself, the belief that she truly had done all she could. It was no good to believe otherwise, not anymore, and so doubts had been shelved, shame tucked away, if only for the few hours that remained.

The knock at the door came and Chloe wished to ignore it, pretend it wasn't there. But out of duty, she answered. At the threshold stood a young man, he held a small silver platter with a wine glass at its center.

"Señora, would you like sherry this evening?"

"I don't believe I ordered this," Chloe said.

"It is complimentary. We offer it on the final night of stay."

"Oh. I see. Gracias."

"May I?" he asked, motioning to enter. The young man placed the glass on the small table next to the flower vase. "I see you are enjoying the flowers," he said. "And they match your beautiful dress."

"Funny, I hadn't noticed," she said. "How did I not notice?"

"Bluebells. Most lovely," he said. "I prefer them in the fields, in the gardens, carpets of them. Here they will die. In the fields, they live, yes?"

"But don't all flowers die in vases eventually?"

"Si, señora. But these come from bulbs, they return each season, forever. We cut them from their roots for you, for this lovely vase, and then they are no more."

"That's sad."

"Ah, but so glorious for you, no?"

"You must have a garden of your own."

"Si. It is small. I am happiest with my hands in dirt. But my wife loves it more. I see her happy. It is my reward."

Chloe thanked the young man again.

"Sleep well tonight, señora."

After the door closed, Chloe sat on the edge of the bed. She wanted to cry but didn't know how. She wanted to scream but knew she could not. She wanted to hear the music at San Miguel Plaza. She wanted to be in Velez Blanco, standing again at the cave, but that, it seemed, was too long ago. At the window again, the lovers gone, she heard only birdsong, a sharp, short, high-pitched cry. She followed the sound across the lawn toward the hill, there on the rocks, a little owl, the owl of Minerva, its plump body illuminated by a dim lamp at the rear of the house. Chloe knew the bird from the mountains, seeing them near the caves before dusk. The owl's plumage was spotted in gray and white, and its flattened face made it appear as if it were frowning. *He is watching me.* She took a sip of the sherry, sweet like raisins, her eyes remaining on the owl, its screeching now silenced. She allowed the wine to linger and then closed her eyes to swallow. When she opened them, the owl had gone.

The night came slowly, the sun setting high on the other side of the grand house. Chloe had promised herself to wait until midnight, in the true darkness when the new day was official. The severe quivers in her legs and behind her eyes, the ones that had come on that morning, had subsided with medicine. She had considered not taking it so that she would be aware to the end of how her body was being ravaged. Instead, she decided to feel as good as she could, to allow nothing, not even her wasting nervous system, to distract her. In time, she knew what was slowly torturing her body would render it frozen. And now, in her fight against the time that would have remained, she was prepared to cut it short and find meaning in hard things, determined to be as conscious to heartbreak, fear, love, and beauty in the last hours. And so, she drank the last of the sherry in tiny sips, allowing it to linger on her tongue, and swallow it with purpose.

Should I pray?

Chloe turned from the window to the bed and remembered her days as a little girl, those nights, kneeling with her clasped hands, her eyes shut, reciting words she did not understand, her dreams lifting to heaven but only floating below its floor. Her mother never spoke of God, of church, but saying her prayers came naturally to Chloe back then. In was in the years after, that she discovered those prayers seemed to go nowhere. Still, in the darkening hotel room, her mind returned to the little girl, the one believing in something greater, the one who knew if she would be good, she could live forever with the man in the clouds. Innocent and trusting, yet shamed if not obedient, if not regretful of her sins. God was not angry, but strict. He was benevolent, kind, but watching and waiting for the mistake a mortal makes. *Was that God or the Church?* It was a question she had asked herself for many years. Which planted the seed of guilt and an endless cry for forgiveness? She longed to be forgiven. Forgiven for everything. Then and now. That is what emerged, and so she dropped to the floor and set her hands in prayer and bowed her head and began to cry in the silence of the lightless room. *There is no resolution,* she thought. *The past is irrevocably gone. It is only memory, that's where it lives, in the fog of a mind trying to understand.* Chloe's heart, without her understanding why, was doing what hearts do, attempt to change the shape she was in, to revive what was lost. *Resolutions are unattainable. They are impossible. Maybe, they are unnecessary.* Chloe's head was now in her hands, and she tasted the salt of her tears, a taste she had always loved. When she had walked in the Granada heat, when her fears had overtaken her, when she had made love, she had tasted the sweat and known she was alive. She stood again at the window to listen for the owl. She leaned into the night but there was nothing, it was too dark. She could hear the chirps of other nightbirds and crickets, but not the owl. She had the owl in her memory. *Memory? Where does it go?* Chloe would die, and her memories would die, too. The pieces of the things that only she owned would eternally vanish. The good and the bad. She could not save them, tuck them away in a bag to be opened when called upon by those left behind. Memories are smoke. *God must be dead.* Still, Chloe believed it was time. She was ready. If she waited, she would regret it. If she hesitated, she would only find more pain—of the body and of the heart.

Chloe stepped away from the window, stretched her arms out from her sides, and began to slowly whirl, the tiny muscles in her naked feet holding to the cold tile to anchor her awkward ballet, her dress twisting with her hips. There was little uncertainty in the movement, the medicine, for now, doing its work. Without it, she knew she would tumble to the ground. *I only wish to feel good.* Chloe began to sing a song she hadn't thought about in years. It surprised her how she had remembered the lyrics. The first lines of Paul McCartney's "Calico Skies," words of fate, and love, and how the angels of love are here to protect us. She could hear McCartney's acoustic guitar, the delicate strums, and his voice, straining a bit in his later years. She sang along with her memory, soft and in time with her dance. And when she could not recall another word, and her body could twist no more, she stepped to the flower vase and bent to the fragrance. There was little to note, and for a moment it saddened her. Bluebells do not offer much to the nose, only the eyes. And maybe that was enough. If they had human qualities, flowers would never be sad for what they were never unable to be, exalting instead in what they were able to give. Flowers are not shamed; they are not guilty. A rose does not long to be an orchid. Chloe's mother loved lilies, she recalled this now. And Chloe loved them, too. Her favorite was the Cana Lily, the golden ones. But the bluebells were not lilies and need not be. Chloe removed a stem from the vase and touched the petals to her cheek, across her jaw, and to the base of her neck next to the pearl of her necklace, holding them there. In time, Chloe knew that the flower's tips would turn white and brown and fall to the ground. *But they will have lived,* she thought, *lamenting nothing.*

Chloe recalled Shakespeare—*Hamlet* and *King Lear* and *Macbeth*—and her mother, and her sister, and the little dog she had as a kid, and the friend she made in 2nd grade, the girl with the thick glasses, and Oregon, and Rainbow Man, and Robert. *May God forgive dear Robert.* She softly kissed the delicate flower and placed the stem in her hair behind her ear, petals at her temple. She sat at the foot of the bed and lowered herself to the sheets, her legs straight, her feet still bare, her arms crossed at the chest, her hands clasped, her fingers intertwined. Above her she saw the white vaulted ceiling and the simple chandelier that held a single bulb throwing no light. With steady breaths, the air releasing from her nose, she felt her pulse at her wrist. And she began to dream, a daydream of a sea voyage, the kind of daydream Chloe had often had in grade school when math bored her and the teacher's words became muted, a voyage far, far away, alone, miles and miles out on the ocean in a small boat that rolled with the waves as it was built to do, and where the wind was all that she needed.

23

While his father was alive, Robert had been to the hunting cabin only once. It was a rundown place built out of timber with room for two twin beds, a small sink and a wood burning stove. A fireplace kept it warm. His father would steal away there with a buddy or two during deer season. Robert remembered how his father would smell when he returned from the Allegheny Mountains—wood smoke, cigars, and sweat. When Robert turned 12 years old, he and his father drove to the cabin together. It was out of season for deer, and that was by design. The trip was solely to show Robert how to handle a rifle.

"You're old enough now. Every boy should know how to shoot," his father said.

The two of them stood together a few dozen yards from the cabin's front door near a strand of pines. His father had a deer rifle and a shotgun, along with bullets and shells. Robert did not want to be there. He did not want to know how to shoot. In Pennsylvania, his father had told him, every boy learns to hunt.

Holding the deer rifle, Robert's father modeled the correct way to stand, how to press the rifle against his shoulder, how to look through the scope, and how pulling the trigger was a squeeze and not a pull. His father fired off one shot into the woods, reloaded and shot another.

"Sometimes getting closer to the ground makes it easier," his father said, falling to one knee and resting his left elbow on his leg.

He fired off another shot. "Ready to try?" his father asked.

Robert offered no expression.

His father dropped in a bullet, handed Robert the rifle, barrel down, and helped to raise the rifle's butt to his son's shoulder. "Hit that tree," his father said, pointing.

Robert looked through the scope.

"Crosshairs, son. When you're ready, squeeze that trigger."

The blast knocked Robert back and off balance. He nearly dropped the rifle.

"Steady yourself," his father said. He reloaded the rifle and handed it back to Robert. "Hit the tree."

Robert missed again but this time was able to keep his body from tumbling over.

"How's that feel?" his father asked.

"It's okay."

"Ready for the shotgun?"

"Isn't it the same?"

Robert knew it wasn't. How could it be? You used a shell not a bullet. And the shotgun was bigger, heavier, deadlier, at least that's how it felt in his hands. He fired into the high branches of the trees, one shot after another.

"Let's try it again," his father said.

Over and over.

Robert wanted to cry. But he didn't. He couldn't.

That day in the woods came to Robert as he walked after midnight through the alleys in the Moroccan market. Most of the shops were closed. But in one of the last remaining open there were several shelves of scarves, leather bags hung from big hooks, and a basket held colorful wool slippers made like tiny sweaters.

Weeks after his father's death, Robert returned to the cabin in the woods. With his mother dead, he had been left to clear it out. It had been more than two years since anyone had been to the cabin. When Robert entered, a field mouse scurried across his shoe. There was the smell of wet wool and mud. On a small table near the bed was an unfinished crossword puzzle from the *Pittsburgh Press* and a white coffee mug with stains inside. On a wooden chair there was an old green blanket, full of holes. On the counter at the sink, a half-full bottle of Canadian Club, and at the foot of one of the beds, his father's slippers, scuffed brown leather. There was little of worth with most everything remaining to be tossed inside a large plastic garbage bag. But Robert was not ready to leave, he opened the old whiskey bottle, sat on one of the beds and tucked his feet into the slippers, and he drank, never minding the time that would pass. *Slippers, such a strange thing,* he thought. Yet he knew. Those slippers had been at the cabin for many years and had been there that long-ago weekend when Robert had learned to shoot and would never shoot again.

His father was a strong man, Built sturdy, bulky. He had boxed as a boy and had listened to the fights on the radio on

Saturday nights. He smoked cigarettes when he was a young man but had quit not long after Robert was born. Drank a bit but Robert remembered seeing his father drunk only once. It was when the Steelers had won the Super Bowl in those golden years. His father liked his steak, and he liked his butter. Oreo cookies with whole milk. And maybe that's what killed him. Clogged arteries, age, and one too many long walks in the woods. His father had never hunted alone. A friend was to join him but became ill and couldn't go, but Robert's father wasn't about to let a beautiful weekend in November go to waste. His body was found two-hundred yards from the cabin, face down in pine needles. One arm under him, the other awkward over his head. His orange vest unbuttoned. His brown hat still on. His deer rifle by his side. The medical examiner said he had been dead for at least a day, maybe longer.

* * *

Robert walked uphill through the market. At the top of the incline was a teahouse, the windows open to the alley. Two old men with long beards smoked from a hookah pipe, the vapor spilling out to the street, sending sweetness into the air. Robert had seen this before here, but at night in the alley, it was more exotic, forbidden. He could not imagine trying it on his own. But the ritual intrigued him, made him curious. He thought about how he might have shared a pipe with Chloe. How she must have tried it before, maybe many times.

What was she doing now? Was it over?

Robert climbed the steps toward the plaza, stopping several times to steady himself. He wasn't drunk, only a bit out of breath. The sangria had gone down easy, but he had mixed the drinks with ham and bread. He could not remember how much wine he had had. It didn't matter. Counting glasses was what Americans do. Near the top of the steps, he turned toward the city. The lights scattered across his view. It was hard to distinguish between those lights and the stars. The horizon had disappeared. His daughter loved the stars. He recalled a night with Debbie when she was young. There was to be a lunar eclipse, and the two of them drove out to the forest an hour away, up in the mountains a few miles from a small ski resort and climbed to a clearing on a hilltop where the sky was black, and they waited and watched, and Robert nearly cried in the experience, and how Debbie did not want to leave until the moon had returned.

In the plaza, a scattering of people sat at tables. Robert could hear talk, conversations in Spanish, most of it soft and low. There was no music tonight. He thought about one more glass of wine, and took a table at Bar Lara, but in a moment, he stood, sighed, and walked to the large doors of the church and looked up to the tiled roof, visible in the night lights. He ran his eyes along the roof line, and down again toward the massive doors. Robert stepped back, found enough balance, and raised his eyes to the tiny cross at the top of the tower.

"Forgive her," he whispered.

Tomorrow he would make the call. Tomorrow he would ask the hotel manager for a wellness check. There had been no word from Chloe since she had gone, just as she said it would be. He wondered what it looked like in her room now. How dark was it? Was there a light left on? Was the window open? Did a breeze fill the room? Did it smell of flowers and perfume? Where was she? In a chair? On the bed? On the cold bathroom floor? Was she wearing the blue dress?

On the walk to the hotel, Robert dodged a speeding moped as it rushed through the narrow streets. He thought for certain the driver would strike something. But it appeared, he had navigated this tight space before. He had no fear; he defied the danger. Robert had come to Spain, he was certain, to find his way out of his own dangers, the wounds inside. And in Spain, he had found avenues out of some of that pain, over and over again, building his own kind of navigational confidence, like the moped driver. But what was in front of him now, what would come tomorrow, was beyond any of this. And as he fumbled with the key to the heavy wooden door of his hotel, Robert began to laugh. *Why? Why am I laughing? Jesus. It must be the wine.* He turned the lock, and the door clunked. He closed the door behind him and despite a delicate touch, it clunked again.

"Buenos noches, señor."

The woman held a broom in her hand and stood near the doorway of the small office on the ground floor. She was young and pretty. Robert could see this even in the low light. She was not the woman he had seen before.

"Hola," Robert said.

"Did you have a good night in our city?" the woman asked.

"I'm not sure," Robert said, now controlling his laugh.

"Ah, but you are smiling, señor. I am certain you will know what made you smile when the sun comes."

"Maybe. Maybe, I will."

The woman returned to her sweeping, and Robert walked through the interior courtyard to his room, unsure of the state he was in.

24

The hotel manager said he had knocked on the door that morning, once and then twice, and had opened it with a master key after there had been no response, calling out as he entered the room. Robert asked what he had found, how it looked. Be specific, Robert insisted. Although he thought the request odd, the manager explained what he had discovered. The window open; the curtains lightly twisted from the breeze. The bed turned down, a pillow with the imprint of a head once resting. In the bathroom, evidence of a shower, water droplets on the tiles. Two white towels had been tossed on the floor. The room key had been left on the bathroom counter.

"Are you sure?" Robert asked.

"Si, señor," the manager said. "There is no one in the room."

"And you looked everywhere?"

"The room is small, señor."

"Can you look again?

The hotel manager placed the phone on his desk and returned to the room. He had not looked in the large clothes closet or under the bed on his first visit, and so now he did, annoyed by Robert's request. As he stood from his knees at the bed, he saw the pill box, the small tin on the nightstand. He held it in his hand, looked at its side and bottom, and shook it. From inside, the clicks of something small. He carried the tin with him to his office, shaking it again. Click. Click.

"She is gone, señor. This is certain. But she did leave an item behind. We can have it posted to her."

"Something behind?"

"A small tin. A pill box, no?"

Robert had been standing, and now he sank to the bed. The phone heavy, like the weight of a stone.

"Señor? Are you there?" the manger asked.

Robert apologized for his silence and for the trouble he had caused. "Throw it out," Robert said. "Toss it away."

"Are you certain, señor? We can have it delivered."

"Get rid of it."

The manager said he would place it with the trash that morning.

"Is there anything else I can do for you, señor?"

Robert offered his phone number and asked that he be contacted if the hotel heard of anything else about the woman, or if the maid found something else in the room, or if there had been a message left at the office that no one had noticed. Robert hung up, tossed the phone on the bed, and dropped his hand to his side, as if he had found relief in letting go. He saw himself in the mirror across the room, the lines at the corners of his eyes, deeper it seemed than before.

* * *

In the hours that passed, the day's heat grew, and Robert adjusted his seat at the table under the umbrella at Bar Lara several times to avoid the sun. He drank red wine and asked one of the waitresses and the owner if they had heard from Chloe. Nothing, they said, reminding Robert that she had taken a few days for a holiday and did not expect to any contact.

A voice came from behind.

"Señor, a gift?"

It was the old woman who sold jewelry, bracelets and necklaces of silver and leather from the basket she carried, the woman who often came to the plaza.

"Have I seen you before, señora?" Robert asked.

The woman smiled. "A gift, no?"

"Not for me."

"Ah, for someone special?"

"I don't think so. Not today."

"There is always time for gifts."

Emma did not wear much jewelry, but Robert bought a locket for her

Birthday in the year after Debbie was born. Inside, the photo of the three of them, the new baby in Emma's arms. He saw that photo quite clearly now.

The old woman held in her palm a simple silver bracelet with a tiny clasp, in the small shape of a flower. "So pretty," she said.

"Muy bueno. But not today, I'm afraid."

"Oh, señor, so beautiful."

Robert's phone rang. It vibrated the tabletop.

"A good price for you, señor," the old woman continued.

On the screen was a number he did not recognize.

"So pretty," the woman said again.

Robert smiled, shook his head, and answered his phone.

There had been a note left at the hotel. It was discovered under the pillow on the bed. The maid had found it as she serviced the room. The hotel manager thought Robert should know.

"Will you read it for me, please?" he asked.

The manager was reluctant but agreed.

Gone to Madrid. The U.S. Embassy. I have stopped running. And even from death, it seems. Maybe what comes now is what the rest of my life is supposed to be about. I'm so sorry. I know this was incredibly hard. I believed it was best that I just go. No more words. Probably best you don't try to contact me. I hope you get this, Robert. I hope you are always happy. To be or not to be, as is said. I guess I chose to be.

Robert was breathless. He wanted to take the next bus to Madrid, he wanted to find her, and at the same time he wanted to forget her, to dismiss everything about her from his every thought. Angry, sad, uncertain, used, lost—all of it swirled in his head. He ended the phone call, and in a state of disbelief, he could only stare to toward the hill that looked out over the city, the blue sky above, empty of clouds. And across the plaza, he saw the old woman who had moved to another table where a young man and a pretty young woman with red hair drank sangria. The old woman had placed the silver bracelet she had shown Robert around the young woman's wrist, and the woman was smiling. The bracelet had found a home.

***

That evening, Robert booked an Air France flight to Lisbon for the morning and then another to New York. A third flight would take him to back home to Pittsburgh. He would land at a reasonable hour, late afternoon local time, a good time for Debbie to pick him up. He placed a pair of socks and underwear on the chair in his room., and on the rack in the closet, he hung a clean white shirt, fresh from the hotel laundry. The pants he wore, the comfortable cotton khakis now frayed at the pocket lines, he would wear again tomorrow. Everything else but his toiletries had been placed inside his bag on the luggage stand near the door. He dampened a handcloth and wiped the inside of his hat, the one he had purchased when he had arrived. Sweat had collected around the brim each day and it had become a habit to wash it and let it dry overnight on the bedpost. Robert placed the hat on his head and stood before the mirror, tilting the hat's brim, posing for an imaginary photo. His skin was brown, tanned, he saw white rings around his eyes where sunglasses had been. Robert moved closer to the mirror and removed the hat. *Who is that man?* He moved closer to his reflection, and notice at his left temple, along the hairline, a blotch about the size of the head of a nine-penny nail, brown in color but not dark. *Was that there before?* He touched it with his fingernail. *A doctor ought to look at that.*

On the bed was the manilla envelope that Chloe had prepared—all the documents, and the key to her apartment. With the plans changed, what to do with it? He thought about tossing it in the large garbage bin at the back of the hotel. He considered packing it and taking it with him. He could leave it at Bar Lara, but there would be too many questions. In time, he was certain he would read about Chloe in the newspaper, see her face on television news as she walked outside important buildings, flanked by men in dark suits. There would be words like *fugitive* and *protests* and *fire* and *Oregon*. And people would talk, and say *it was about time*, and find her story despicable, and call her a coward, and a crazy, and a communist. And prosecutors would demand life in prison and maybe the death penalty. And maybe in time, Robert would say he knew her, he once knew that woman who ran and hid away in faraway places, and maybe someday he will tell people that they didn't understand her story and that maybe, maybe there was more to everything, more to tell.

* * *

It was late, too late for anything, he thought. Still, Robert craved a beer. He hadn't had one in a long time. He could almost taste his favorite, Rolling Rock. But even a lowly Iron City sounded good, a beer from home, one he could drink from a can while listening to the Pirates on the radio. And so, he washed water over his face and brushed his teeth. He raised his hands above his head and stretched, reaching as high as he could. He closed his eyes and rolled his head on his neck. *A beer and good fried fish. That's what I need.* Robert remembered the beer-battered Fridays at the VFW hall, and how he and Emma would make a date of it, sitting together with their fish and their beer at one of the Formica top tables in the hall. *What would Hemingway do?* Robert thought. After all, Robert had come to Spain with Hemingway dreams. He recalled an article he had read before his trip about Hemingway's favorite haunts in Spain, and one was a German beer house in Madrid. A beer joint in Spain seemed an odd thing, but Hemingway loved the place. And so, that is what Robert wanted, a beer and Pescaíto frito.

On this way out to the street, Robert stopped at the open hotel office door. Inside was the older woman who had checked him in when he first arrived.

"Hola, señor," she said, standing from the desk.

"I don't have any messages, do I? No one has tried to reach me?"

The woman searched a small stack of papers on her desk. "Hmm, I do not think so, señor." She looked in the slotted shelves to her left where the room keys were kept. "Nothing that I see. Were you expecting something, señor?"

Robert shook his head.

"If something does come in, I will be sure to write it down and slide it under your door. Would that be good, señor?"

"Si. Gracias."

"Or course, señor. Is there anything else I can do for you?"

Robert thought for a moment. "Yes. There is. Where at this late hour could I find the best fried fish and the coldest beer in Granada?"

25

Sleep was unreliable over the ocean, and now on the last leg from New York, a young man, a college student on summer break, took the seat next to Robert and wanted to talk as much as Robert wanted quiet, to disappear.

"I thought the Statue of Liberty was going to be bigger than it was, but I liked The Village and the little shops and the good Italian food."

"Ah huh." Robert said, attempting to be polite.

"Ever been to The White Horse Tavern? You know, the place where Dylan Thomas drank himself to death?"

"No. I haven't."

"One of those geeky things to do if you're into it. And I'm an English literature major, so."

Robert leaned his head against the window and closed his eyes, hoping the young man would get the hint.

"Who's your favorite writer?" the student asked.

"Hemingway," Robert mumbled, his eyes remaining closed.

"I like the short stories. Right? Have you read them?

"Ah huh."

"What's your favorite novel of his? It's not the one everybody picks, even though it won those awards, but I just love *The Old Man and the Sea*. It's really a fable, right? So compact and deep. Right?"

"Hmm. Hmm."

"I think we'll be landing soon. So, you might want to put your seat up."

Robert's mouth opened slightly, and his breathing slowed. He was now in the in-between, the space amid awake and asleep, in the foggy place of the inexplicable and uncertain.

"Mister?' the student asked. He leaned close and said again, "Mister?"

The plane turned and through the window came the slants of filtered sunlight, creating flashes of shadows across Robert's closed eyes, stirring him.

"Are we home?" Robert murmured.

"The attendants are walking the aisle. We're close, yeah."

Out the window Robert saw green hills and little houses on their tiny plots below. The plane banked and its wing lifted toward the slate sky, and Robert was suddenly unbalanced, his stomach uneasy, equilibrium momentarily lost. He heard the growl of the plane's wheels lowering into position below him, preparing for landing, and he was now unsettled.

"Pittsburgh, right?"

"Minutes away."

"I don't even remember New York. And we left Spain, what, last night, this morning? What time is it here?"

The student showed Robert his wristwatch. "I adjusted the time at JFK," he said.

Robert's long trip, all of it, had lost its vividness. In the murkiness of awakening, he could recall none of it in any precise way. All of it in a cloud, grainy images replacing the sharpness of recent memory. Yet he knew the days had altered him; he knew he was different.

Through the gate and the terminal to baggage claim, Robert passed the hotdog kiosk, the tiny bars, and restaurants where passengers waited and drank overpriced beer and ate packaged chicken salads from plastic containers, passed the luggage shop, the popcorn stand, and the teenage girls sitting on the floor near the restrooms, scrolling through their phones, drinking through straws from large plastic cups from Smoothie King. From the speakers somewhere above him, music played a string orchestra version of "Let it Be." All of it so ordinary.

At the bottom of the escalator, Robert searched for familiar faces. He spotted the young man from the plane and followed him to baggage claim number 11. The carousel clunked into motion, but for several minutes there was nothing to see. Robert watched in silence as the conveyor moved round and round and round. He looked at his phone screen. A text from Debbie. *B there in 15.* An unexpected sense of remorse came over Robert, a level of regret, of something lost. He stood in a kind of purgatory, it seemed, in between angels and demons, and coming home would not soon change things.

The young man from the plane had moved close to Robert's side. "Hey, I never asked you." he said as they waited for the luggage. "Where do you live around here?"

"Mt. Washington," Robert said.

"Oh wow, I love it up there. Took my girlfriend up to see the city lights at night last Christmas. My parents live in Murrysville. That's where I'm going. For now."

"I like Murrysville."

"When I graduate, I want to move to Colorado. Hope to travel first. Backpack Europe or something. Spain, right? That's where you were, right? Did you like the people there?"

For a moment Robert did not know how to answer, and the heaviness of regret fell on him. "There are good people there. Very good people," he said. "Go see the world, young man. It's a big, big world to see."

Home is where Robert stood now. The airport only two dozen miles from his front door. This was his hometown, where he became what he was, where he fell in love, where he found peaceful days and nights of solace, and gratitude.

"That's me," the young man said, spotting his canvas duffel bag on the carousel. He pulled it close and threw the strap over his shoulder. "Maybe I'll see you again sometime on a flight out here. I don't know, Africa, Italy, Tangier, right?" The young man saluted Robert, like a soldier, and stepped toward the sliding doors that led to the outside. He stopped for a moment and turned back. "By the way, I really like the hat," he said. "It looks good on you, you know?"

Robert held the crown and adjusted the hat, lowering the brim to just above his eyes. "Spain," he said. "First day." And he waved goodbye.

Robert stood with his bag at his side along the concrete sidewalk a few dozen yards from the hotel bus kiosk. Cars angled their way from one lane to another, all moving in the same direction, as waiting passengers stretched on their tiptoes, hoping to see their rides. A young woman, sitting on her large suitcase, stood when she heard a car horn and waved to the driver of a blue SUV. He smiled. She did, too. They hugged at the vehicle's open hatch. He kissed her. *Happy people,* Robert thought.

Robert's phone buzzed.

Close. At the corner.

He lifted his bag from the pavement and stepped to the sidewalk's edge. In the near distance of the inside lane, he spotted Debbie's car. As it moved closer, he could see her face, examining the crowd. Robert waved his hand high above his head. *It's the hat,* he realized. *She doesn't recognize me in the hat.*

"Debbie!"

Her eyes caught his, but there was no recognition.

"Honey, it's me!"

Debbie was about to pull away and return the car to the stream of traffic when Robert stepped from the curb.

"Honey!"

The car lurched and stopped. For a long moment, Debbie, with two hands gripping the top of the steering wheel, sat staring. She blinked and blinked again. Scientists say recognition first comes to us in a few thousandths of a second and remains for a lifetime. For Debbie on that evening, in that split second, science did not matter. The man before her was someone changed.

She pulled over and stepped from the car.

"My goodness. I almost hit you. You've got to watch out, stepping off the curb like that, Dad."

"Hey, honey."

"Is this all of it?" she asked, taking Robert's bag from his hand.

"All there is."

Debbie hugged her father. "And what's with the hat?" she asked.

"You don't like it?"

"Oh, Dad," she smiled. "Welcome home."

She returned to the driver's seat and turned the car toward the row of cars. Debbie touched her father's knee. "Flight okay? You tired? You must be hungry?"

Robert watched the red flash of brake lights on the car ahead, the driver slowly maneuvering through the exit lane. And beyond the car, the rumble of a bus accelerating from its stop, black smoke spewing into the air. He heard a jet engine above and from the open window of an adjacent car, a song on the radio, spilling out to the late afternoon.

"Who sang that? That song. Do you remember that?"

Debbie waved to the traffic officer who'd allowed space in the tide of vehicles to permit her to merge into the left lane. In the flow of traffic, she said, "I'm sorry, Dad. What did you say?"

The car was gone, and so was the music.

"That song. I haven't heard that in years."

"I'm sorry. I didn't notice."

Adjusting the seat to allow him to lean further back, Robert was less adrift than he had been on the long flight and at baggage claim. But he was suddenly disappointed that he had not asked more questions of the student on his flight, more about his studies, his longing for travel. *I should have paid more attention.* With his neck against the head rest, he decided that as soon as he could, he would return to Bingham Tavern and order a Rock and tell the bartender all about the old matador he met in Seville. And if the sun was shining tomorrow, and the Pirates were in town, he would wear his new hat to the ball game and sing the National Anthem and stand during the seventh-inning stretch and hope for a foul ball to come his way. And then he would go home, and he would tend to his lawn and maybe plant marigolds along the walkway for the first time in many years. And he would stay up late and have a glass of red wine and return to all those books that remained on his reading list.

"It's good to be home," Robert said, watching the green hills emerge above the road on the horizon.

"I'm happy you're home, too, Dad," Debbie said.

Robert closed his eyes and inhaled.

"So," Debbie said, "tell me all about Spain."

The airport road lifted toward the highway and in the southern sky, the clouds darkened, shades of gray swirling together.

Soon, it would begin to rain.

About the Author

DAVID W. BERNER is the author of eight books. His work has been recognized by the Society of Midland Authors, the Chicago Writers Association, the Eric Hoffer Book Awards, and the Royal Dragonfly Book Awards. David has also been honored as the Writer-in-Residence at the Jack Kerouac Project in Florida, and at the Ernest Hemingway Birthplace Home and Museum in Illinois. He lives outside Chicago.